Diamond Head

A Miss Danforth Mystery

Diamond Head

Marian J. A. Jackson

Walker and Company
New York

First published in the United States of America in 1992
by Walker Publishing Company, Inc.

Published simultaneously in Canada by Thomas Allen & Son
Canada, Limited, Markham, Ontario

Library of Congress Cataloging-in-Publication Data
Jackson, Marian J. A.
Diamond head / Marian J. A. Jackson.
p.   cm.
ISBN 0-8027-1247-9
I. Title. II. Series: Jackson, Marian J.A. Miss Danforth mystery.
PS3560.A228D53   1992
813'.54—dc20   92-16867
CIP

Printed in the United States of America
2 4 6 8 10 9 7 5 3 1

For
Julie, Jon, and Winterchild
I love you

Acknowledgments

It is only by having free (except for the expenses of the trip) access to the treasures in the Hawaiian Public Library System and Archives, and the friendly librarians who patiently answered my many questions, that I was able to write this book. Thank you for being there. A special thanks to Richard Marks, unofficial historian of Kalaupapa, Molokai, for his generosity and unique insight.

I am immensely grateful to my agent, Elizabeth Backman, for all of her efforts on my behalf, and to my editor, Michael Seidman.

Glossary of Hawaiian Words

Aloha   Either hello or good-bye, welcome or farewell, it can also mean romantic love, affection, or best wishes

Apikela   Abigail

Haole   A white foreigner, someone who cannot trace their ancestors to the beginning of the world

Kahuna   A powerful man of the gods, either for good or evil

Kapu   Forbidden, taboo

Lanai   A porch or veranda

Lau hala   Weaving of hats, mats, etc. from the prepared fronds of the pandanus (screw pine)

Luna   Overseer, or foreman of a plantation

Mahalo nui   Big thanks or thank you very much

Mai paki	Leprosy, Hansen's Disease, or the Chinese Disease
Makai	Toward the sea (when giving directions)
Mauka	Toward the mountains (when giving directions)
Pau hana	After work
Poi	A paste made from pounding the taro root
Punee	A narrow bed or couch
Tapa	Cloth made from beaten bark
Ti	A broad-leafed plant used for many purposes, from wrapping food to hula skirts
Wahine	Young woman, female, girl

Cast of Characters
(In Order of Appearance)

Abigail Patience Danforth, the world's first female
consulting detective

Maude Cunningham, Abigail's companion and former
client

Jacqueline Bordeaux, Abigail's personal maid

Kinkade, Abigail's majordomo

Princess Lilliana, a cousin of deposed Hawaiian royalty

William, friend of Princess Lilliana

Yasushi Miamoto, Japanese servant in the
Tarkingtons' household

Penelope Tarkington, daughter of Abner Tarkington

Matthew Tarkington, son of Abner Tarkington

Drew Miller, police officer

Abner Tarkington, wealthy sugar baron and
ex-missionary

Bruce Dalton, friend of the Tarkingtons

a kahuna lapa'au, a powerful Hawaiian healer

Various speaking parts and walk-ons

▽

1

"MATTHEW TARKINGTON?" ABIGAIL'S EYES grew dark with suspicion. "Why, pray, must I see him?" Seating herself in the ornate wicker armchair opposite Maude, she automatically arranged the folds of her voluminous skirt so that it fell most becomingly. Her piercing gaze never left her companion's face.

Even without Abigail's scrutiny, gowned as she was in heavy widow's weeds, the heat of the tropical afternoon would have caused Maude discomfort. Thus she had chosen the lanai on the west side of the Royal Hawaiian Hotel for its dependable breeze, and privacy, for their rendezvous. Her gray eyes did not flinch from Abigail's sharp gaze. "A most engaging young man, is he not?" Knowing she might incur Abigail's ire, she nonetheless risked a rare smile as she continued, "And as heir to his father's sugar holdings, soon to be rich?"

"Drivel!" Abigail exclaimed, furious that Maude dared play the matchmaker. "You above all should know—"

"Forgive me, Miss Danforth." Maude leaned forward to touch Abigail's wrist and forestall further protest. "For in sooth, I jest."

Dislodging Maude's hand with an impatient shake of her

own, Abigail's eyes narrowed dangerously. "My forswearing emotion to preserve the integrity of my intellect is not a matter for you, or anyone else, to take lightly!"

"It is for Mr. Tarkington's sake that I apologize, Miss Danforth," Maude replied, instantly regretting her attempt at levity. These past few weeks in the lush paradise of Oahu had done nothing to improve Abigail's strange lassitude, and she could but hope that the prospect of a crime to solve might restore her young friend's normal enthusiasm. Or at the very least improve her testy disposition. "I took the liberty of telling his sister how cleverly you had solved my beloved Charles's murder."

Abigail closed her eyes. "An overlarge woman in a ghastly flowered gown—" she said, opening her eyes to gaze coolly at Maude. "Miss Penelope Tarkington, I do believe."

"The very one," Maude replied, impressed anew at Abigail's memory. They had met scores of people at the Daltons', and to her certain knowledge Abigail had not engaged Penelope in conversation beyond a nod of acknowledgment on being introduced. "Upon the conclusion of our tête-à-tête, she seemed to believe that you could help her brother."

Only by subtle lift of brow did Abigail betray that she had heard Maude, and that she awaited further comment.

Maude shivered inwardly at Abigail's stern visage. Her Gibson-girl profile had been chiseled clean. The wasp-waisted vogue of the 1900s had always suited Abigail's slender figure, but Jacqueline had surely been obliged to tighten her mistress's corset by several notches to accommodate a weight loss. Abigail had professed a dislike for the exotic cuisine of the islands, but Maude was convinced that the very stifling of her emotions of which she was so proud had robbed Abigail of her accustomed appetite for living as well as for food. "Miss Tarkington suspects her brother is in grave danger," she continued solemnly.

"Oh, come now, Miss Cunningham!"

Abigail stood. With an angry rustle of skirts, she strode to the railing that overlooked yet another garden. She found the profusion of blossoms and their riotous colors somewhat vulgar, not in the least like a proper English garden. Wanton fragrances threatened to make her giddy, and the incessant chatter of birdsong preyed upon her nerves. Turning her back to the view, she faced Maude. In the imperious manner of her father she continued, "Either he is in danger, or he is not!"

"Perhaps if I told you the particulars, you could decide?"

Abigail's curt nod was all the encouragement that Maude received.

"Pray understand, Miss Danforth," Maude continued swiftly since Abigail seemed poised for flight, "it was only after I had told her of your success that she confided in me. And even then she spoke with great reluctance."

Abigail looked at Maude askance, her tone ominous. "Why does she not approach me directly?"

Maude's patience, which was thin at best, began to fray at Abigail's haughty demeanor, and her tone was more harsh than wise when she said, "Apparently her brother vowed not to give you another chance to rebuff him after his last attempt to engage you in conversation at dinner—"

"Fanny feathers!" Abigail interrupted, an innocent hand to her breast. "I rebuffed him—?"

"Yes!" Maude nodded for emphasis. "She feared Mr. Tarkington might accuse her of interfering and therefore implored me to intervene."

Insulted beyond measure, Abigail drew herself tall. "I assure you I am infallibly kind when informing an unwanted suitor that his attention is unwelcome."

Abigail's protest was more than Maude could bear. Forgetting her mission, she replied with some heat, "If you continue to persist in your rude behavior toward every gentleman who finds you comely, you will end up an unbearable old maid—"

"You're a fine one to talk!" Abigail shook an accusing finger at Maude as she stepped away from the railing.

Maude stood. "At least I have known the love of a man."

"I will not engage in this same tiresome quarrel, Miss Cunningham." Again, Abigail's skirts rustled angrily as she started for the French doors leading to the hotel.

Realizing she had defeated herself, Maude was immediately contrite. "Oh, I pray you, do not leave, Miss Danforth," she said, moving quickly to reach Abigail's side. "I do apologize for straying from my purpose."

Impressed by the beseeching expression in Maude's eyes, and not a little surprised by her second apology, since she seldom indulged in the practice, Abigail paused in midstride.

Maude extended her hand to indicate the chairs they had vacated.

Sighing heavily, Abigail took her seat, and once again arranged her skirts.

Maude leaned forward and spoke in a conspiratorial manner. "While brushing his hair before going to the Daltons', Mr. Tarkington dropped his hairbrush."

Abigail rolled her eyes heavenward as if asking for deliverance, and groaned.

Before Abigail could gain her feet, Maude grasped her wrist and, holding it against the arm of her chair with a firm grip, continued earnestly, "He has begun experiencing a tingling of his shinbones." Still gripping Abigail's arm, she swiftly looked about to be certain they were alone before lowering her voice to a whisper. "The soles of his feet sometimes itch, and no amount of scratching will stop it."

Abigail wrenched her arm away in disgust. "Mr. Tarkington needs a doctor, not a consulting detective," she said, rubbing her wrist.

"Nay, Miss Danforth." Maude shook her head emphatically. "They fear doctors above all others."

"And why might that be?" Abigail asked with an annoyed frown.

Again, Maude looked about to ensure their continued privacy. Leaning forward, she whispered, "Molokai!"

Abigail's eyes widened with horror. "Leprosy?" The instant the word escaped her lips, she clapped her hand over her mouth, and also looked about to see if she'd been overheard. In spite of her resolve, her heart went out to Mr. Tarkington. However his symptoms had begun, he would soon stink of his own putrefying flesh, doomed to live in a slowly rotting body until death mercifully released him. No cure existed. As if the disease itself were not horrific enough, fear of *mai paki* was so great, the slightest hint of its onslaught and the hapless victim was, by law, automatically and irrevocably banished to live the rest of his days in hell— the leper colony on the island of Molokai. "Is she quite sure?" Abigail asked, her voice husky with sympathy. "Her brother's symptoms could stem from any number of benign afflictions."

"That very question is the reason she seeks your help—"

"But a doctor—?"

"Doctors must report such inquiries to the authorities— the very suspicion would place him at risk—"

"Surely his family physician?—the one who treats the father—?"

Maude leaned forward and whispered. "Miss Tarkington fears her brother is being poisoned."

"Why did you not tell me so at once?" Abigail replied, her eyes alight with interest.

"I have been making a most earnest attempt to do so for the last five days—"

Abigail drew herself tall. "Just what is it you imply, Miss Cunningham—"

"I imply nothing, Miss Danforth!" With no little effort, Maude repressed her desire to remind Abigail just how frigid her demeanor had been any time Matthew Tarkington's name had been mentioned since the Daltons' party. Instead, she leaned forward in a conspiratorial manner, her voice free of censure as she said, "It is rumored that some physicians will fake a diagnosis for a price."

"Diabolical!" Abigail shuddered. "Have they any notions about the identity of the culprit?"

Maude pulled back. "I did not presume to ask—"

"The question is elementary, Miss Cunningham!" Abigail replied with a reproving frown.

"I felt those inquiries were better left to an expert, Miss Danforth," Maude said sincerely. "If, of course, you should decide to take Mr. Tarkington's part in the matter."

Brow raised appraisingly, Abigail glanced at her companion, and sighed. "Just as well you did not ask." She shrugged. "You might well have botched it." Recalling how difficult it had been to extract information from Maude regarding the circumstances of Charles's death, her tone was ironic as she continued, "I myself have experienced no little difficulty in gleaning facts from reluctant witnesses—"

The irony was lost on Maude as she hastened to ask, "Then you will take Mr. Tarkington's case?" She leaned forward eagerly. Although Abigail's gaze was now fixed upon the garden, Maude could tell that the young detective's thoughts were occupied, and resisted her impulse to press for an immediate answer.

At last Abigail spoke. "I have long thought murder to be the most dastardly crime possible." She glanced at Maude. "Mr. Tarkington's dire situation would have me revise that conclusion." She stood and looked up, her glance raking the facade of the hotel. In that brief observation, she caught a glimpse of a door moving. Unable to tell whether it was shutting, the listener disappearing inside with their secret, or about to open, she quickly put out her hand to prevent Maude from speaking. Heart thumping wildly, she froze.

Twisting about in her chair, Maude followed Abigail's gaze.

Both ladies immediately relaxed when the diminutive Jacqueline emerged in a dress unadorned by apron. A straw hat anchored flat upon her head and white gloves upon her hands indicated that she was prepared to leave the hotel.

"Have you not yet learned to knock?" Abigail called out sharply, annoyed with herself for having been so thoroughly alarmed at so small a cause.

Even though she'd been uncertain of the protocol, rather than disturb her betters in a private conversation, Jacqueline had tried to make her presence known, but the huge doors had absorbed the tiny sound she'd been able to make, which at best would have been too weak to be heard in a modest room, much less an open veranda wherein the chatter of birds competed with the rustle of leaves disturbed by a constant breeze. Already upset by the necessity of seeking out her mistress, and rattled by the injustice of Abigail's uncommon impatience, Jacqueline's flawed English failed her as she approached them.

"Well, what do you want?" Irritated by her maid's interruption as well as her silence, Abigail sat once again, requiring Jacqueline to circle their chairs and stand with her back to the railing so that she could face her mistress as she spoke.

"Beg pardon, Miss Danforth, Miss Cunningham." Clutching her reticule in both hands in front of her, Jacqueline nodded at each in turn. "Might Monsieur Kinkade be away at the errand for you?"

Abigail glanced at Maude suspiciously, wondering if she had presumed to give Kinkade orders without consulting her.

Maude shook her head in an indignant denial.

Abigail turned her attention to Jacqueline. "Why do you ask?"

"It is my afternoon free, thank you, miss. He takes me to the city so I do not lose myself." An eloquent shrug was testimony to her efforts to find him as she continued, "He is no place in the hotel."

"Where had you planned to meet?" Abigail asked.

Jacqueline released one hand from its grip on her reticule to indicate the far side of the hotel. "By the bicycles—"

"Bicycles?" Maude interrupted. "When did you learn how to ride?"

"I have no learning so far, Miss Cunningham," Jacqueline said. "Monsieur Kinkade, he promises to teach me," she continued eagerly. Ever since they had disembarked at the wharf, he had made himself scarce. Her duties had kept her close to Abigail, or the sewing box when Abigail was out, yet he seemed to always be off on some task away from the hotel. When he reappeared, he was distracted, unlike himself, and she had been looking forward to discovering what had transpired to effect such a change. Lest the ladies suspect her true motive, she quickly added, "He says riding to see the sights is faster than walking, and saves much time."

"True enough—" Abigail began.

"Do you think it wise that Jacqueline ride about a strange city upon a bicycle?" Maude's question overrode Abigail's response. "What if she were to fall and break her arm? Where would you be if you had to take care of your maid instead of the other way around?" Turning to Jacqueline, she added, "Did you ask Miss Danforth for permission?"

Jacqueline hung her head. "No, miss." It had not occurred to her that she should have cleared what she did on her own time with Abigail. As long as her behavior brought no discredit to the household—if the four of them could be considered a household, since they were guests at a hotel and not occupying a real house—she had assumed that she could do as she liked. Desperately sorry that she had mentioned the subject, Jacqueline held her breath for her mistress's response. Should Abigail forbid bicycle riding, she would be forced to use the streetcar since she despised riding horseback, Abigail kept no carriage, and hacks, even a dog cart, were too dear when she knew no one with whom to share.

"Stuff and nonsense!" Abigail exclaimed. Although she disliked contradicting Maude in front of a servant, this time her companion had gone too far with her squeamishness. And she certainly did not want Jacqueline underfoot during her time off. Traveling with servants was proving to be awkward. Not so much Jacqueline, since her duties were clear, and essential, and could easily be expanded. But Kinkade was another matter, especially in Honolulu where all male houseservants were dark skinned, be they Japanese, Portuguese, Hawaiian, or some such—never white. She had even considered renting a house if they were to stay much longer so that Kinkade could at least be put to work in a garden. Or better yet, move on to a place where he would not be such an oddity, since letting him go was out of the question no matter the inconvenience. The whirl of the town had long since begun to pall. Only now there was the inkling of a mystery to unravel in Mr. Tarkington's dilemma. If Kinkade could be occupied a few hours teaching Jacqueline a useful skill, why not? With a glance at Maude that brooked no disagreement, she said, "The only difficulty I foresee is finding a cycle small enough."

Thoroughly annoyed by Abigail's cavalier attitude toward the obvious dangers involved in Jacqueline's headstrong pursuit, Maude folded her arms, fixed her gaze upon the garden, and withdrew from the conversation.

"Kinkade is usually quite punctual," Abigail continued. "Perhaps if you sought him again at the bicycle stand he might be there by now?"

"Yes, miss," Jacqueline responded with alacrity. She all but flew to the doors before the dour Miss Cunningham could find her voice again and quash her outing.

Chattering birds and agitated leaves filled the silence when Abigail grew as quiet as Maude upon Jacqueline's departure. At length, Maude slowly lifted her arms about her head in a languid stretch, and spoke. "Well, Miss Danforth?" she drawled.

"Well—what, Miss Cunningham?"

Maude quelled her mounting temper. "Will you help Mr. Tarkington?"

Abigail sighed. "I was about to say—before we were so rudely interrupted—that I had reached a conclusion." She paused a moment before continuing solemnly, "There are indeed fates worse than death."

"Then I shall telephone Miss Tarkington at once." Maude started to rise.

"Do not be so hasty." Abigail held out a restraining hand. "It would not do to seem overeager to engage myself."

"Then I have not done Miss Tarkington's difficulty full

justice," Maude replied earnestly. "She needs must have the answer to the true state of her brother's health before her father dies."

Abigail did not bother to disguise the impatience she felt. "When you earlier made reference to Matthew Tarkington's inheritance, did you actually mean that their father is near death?"

"The doctors have told Miss Penelope that his heart grows weaker with every passing day."

"Does he know about his son's—ah—condition?"

Maude shook her head. "The news would kill him."

"Poor Miss Penelope." Abigail sighed with sympathy. "What trials."

"You would not know it to speak with her," Maude said, a touch of awe in her voice. "Such a noble soul. Her fate is bleak indeed."

Fearing a descent into mawkish sentiment, Abigail drew herself tall. "Aside from the great losses she must endure, of course, the lady will be well fixed—"

"Not so, Miss Danforth," Maude interrupted. "That is why she needs you so desperately."

Abigail struck the arm of her chair. "Must you keep me in mystery?"

"Lepers have no rights," Maude responded swiftly. "Should Matthew inherit his father's vast holdings and be found to have the disease, his entire fortune would revert to the state. Miss Tarkington would be left penniless."

Abigail could not believe her ears. "She could not inherit?"

"Matthew Tarkington would be shorn of his rights because of the technicality of the property's being in his name at the time of his commitment to Molokai."

"But that is monstrous!" Abigail exclaimed.

"Now can you see why that dear lady is so desperate for your help?"

Abigail stood, and strode to the railing. As she stared into the garden, she wondered what sinister forces had aligned themselves against Penelope Tarkington. With such a large fortune at stake, the culprit must be a master of deceit and, given the ghastly fate of Matthew Tarkington, pitiless. At length, she turned to face Maude. "And I shall help her, Miss Cunningham," Abigail said, her voice firm with resolve. "Come!" She held out her hand to Maude. "Let us make that telephone call."

$\triangledown$

2

F<small>OR ALL HIS WORLDLY</small> travels, Kinkade was not a worldly man. But as valet to Abigail's father, he had acquired a certain expertise in escorting his charges and their baggage through the intricacies of arrival at a new port of call, and it was not without pride that, rather than have them tarry in the blazing sun on the treeless wharf, he had enabled his mistress, Miss Cunningham, and Jacqueline, burdened only by sweet-smelling leis that had been placed about their necks by smiling strangers, to embark immediately upon their journey to the hotel. They'd had no need to bother their heads about such details as taxes for the Queen's Hospital, permits for their luggage, or locating the hotel's carriage among the tangle of gigs, sulkies, spring wagons, surreys, and barouches parked every which way so that hundreds of babbling folk of every hue imaginable could descend and greet the newcomers.

Attuned as he was to fashion, all the while he was thus engaged he could not help but note with disdain that most men wore out-of-fashion bowlers, while the ladies favored an unbecoming flat-brimmed straw to top their unfashionably flowered prints. He did not, however, disapprove of the gingham that seemed favored for young girls, or the caps and knee britches sported by the Fauntleroys. Shapeless garments he'd not seen before, and would not care to again, if asked, covered the native women like tents. Having never before seen so much as a lady's fully booted ankle, except when accidentally exposed to the great embarrassment of its owner, he was deeply shocked, if not offended, to note that they were barefoot. He blushed to think what the bare-chested Hawaiian boys had worn while diving for the pennies the passengers had tossed overboard.

A great coral reef protected the small harbor, and although he'd been impressed by the grace of the many-arched public storehouses, and solid-stone custom house, he had been disappointed by the much-touted Diamond Head. Bursting straight up from the ocean floor to pierce the sky, its majesty was lost on him since it failed to sparkle the way he'd been led to believe it should. The fabled sailor who had thought he'd seen diamonds must have been in his cups. Even in the midday sun, it was dusty brown blotched with green. The name was deceitful, and he felt cheated.

His charges successfully dispatched toward the shady hills, he had found the hotel's dray and, baggage on board, crossed the driver's palm, thus persuading him to wait until the stock had been unloaded. While he might have taken pride in his skill in serving his betters, it rankled mightily that he was expected to watch after Abigail's horse. Admittedly, he had grown fond of Crosspatches these last few months, but he deeply resented being cast in the role of stable hand. His cravat threatened to choke him in the sweltering heat, and it was only professional pride that kept him from loosening it. No need to embarrass Miss Danforth by looking like a common stevedore. His nose, broken in his youth, had toughened his face so that he naturally more nearly resembled a man who earned his living in a rough trade rather than as a gentleman's gentleman.

Unbeknownst to Kinkade, Crosspatches had already been safely delivered to the paddock and was milling about with the cattle like a king among commoners, attracting much attention since fine horseflesh was greatly appreciated on the islands, with hotly contested races at Kapioloni Park a weekly event. By the time Kinkade discovered, and retrieved, the thoroughbred, he was terribly thirsty, and intent upon a drink of cool water, or perhaps an iced lemonade at the hotel. He therefore gave short shrift to the curious who would impede his progress with their questions, and ignored those who braved his taciturn demeanor to follow him as he led Crosspatches to the dray. He was hitching the horse to the back of the vehicle when a melodious voice interrupted his concentration. Looking up, an ill-tempered retort upon his lips, his anger, along with this thirst, vanished in the liquid brown gaze of the most beautiful girl he had ever seen. Her tawny skin glowed with health, and her lustrous fine hair, crowned by colorful blossoms, flowed unimpeded down her back. Rather than cover her like a tent, her native garment hinted at a lithe shapeliness. Unsupported by corset, her carriage was nonetheless regal. Unable to control his curiosity, he glanced down. Confirming that her feet were indeed bare, his face turned crimson to the roots of his hair.

"Aloha, Mr.—?" She smiled an invitation for him to supply his name.

Whipping his hat off, he bowed slightly. "Kinkade at your service, Miss—?" His smile transformed his rough features as he returned a like invitation.

"Princess Lilliana," she replied, stroking the delighted thoroughbred on the nose. "And your horse?"

"Crosspatches, ma'am—I mean to say—Princess." He was about to explain that the horse belonged to Miss Danforth, but she turned her attention toward her several friends who had gathered close when the stern-looking man had deigned to speak to her. All admired the splendid horse except for one enormous, scowling fellow who insinuated himself between the princess and Kinkade.

The princess sidestepped him with an uncommon grace. "An interesting name for a horse, Mr. Kinkade," she said casually, ignoring her large companion, who hid his displeasure by stroking the horse. Before Kinkade could find his tongue, she continued, "Have you imported him for the races?"

The large one glared at Kinkade, the furrow between his brows deepening. She turned again to her friends. They practiced Crosspatches's name, admired his deep chest, and speculated upon his speed amid politely smothered giggles.

Kinkade's desire to correct her assumptions that the horse was his or that he belonged to the ranks of the well-heeled racing crowd, and a search for words to explain how the horse had gotten his name all tangled with a fierce desire to strike the large fellow upon the nose. The resultant logjam, along with her inattention, rendered him speechless.

Again, she turned to him before he could speak. "Perhaps we will meet again at the track?"

Utterly unprepared for her question, he could but speak his heart. "It is devoutly to be wished, Princess—"

"Aloha—till then?" Her radiant smile left him breathless. Before he could respond, she had turned to her friends and, except for the large disgruntled one who shot daggers at Kinkade, they departed in a flurry of merriment.

As he gazed after her retreating figure, the enormity of his deception hit him like a blow to the jaw from the large one. Yet he knew he must see her again, even if it meant living a lie.

The very day he was to meet Jacqueline at the bicycles, he was at the blacksmith's discussing what he considered an overcharge with the smithy, when a great hullabaloo interrupted their budding argument. Curious, he went to the entrance to see what caused the racket.

Wailing like banshees, thwacking horses, donkeys, and jackasses to greater effort, male and female dark-hued riders, garbed in every conceivable color, flew by J. J. Hansen's Smithy, kicking up a fearful dust storm.

"Pay them no mind," J. J. called after him. "Happens every Saturday. *Pau hana*—after work—them Hawaiians mount whatever's got four legs, and tear around town scaring decent folk half to death."

"Can you not stop them?" Kinkade asked, slapping at his trousers with his gloves, wishing for a whisk broom.

"Some customs die hard." J. J. shrugged.

As the last of the riders sped past, before rejoining Mr. Hansen, Kinkade looked past the row of seated graybeards selling *lau hala* fans and mats from the shaded sidewalk to see what four-legged creatures the stragglers might be mounted on. His heart lurched in his chest when he instantly recognized the Princess Lilliana standing on the corner, poised to cross the street. Without a second thought for the consequences, he waved to attract her attention.

Although she was looking in his direction, she did not see him.

Forgetting his errand, Kinkade stepped into the street, intent upon intercepting her before she reached the other side.

Not seeing the reason for Kinkade's sudden disappearance, J. J. opened his mouth to call after him. Remembering the nature of Kinkade's visit, he thought better of it, shrugged, and returned to his anvil.

Still waving, Kinkade had gained the street by the time the princess recognized him. Her smile stopped his heart altogether. In an effort to regain his composure he looked beyond her, and gasped. A riderless horse, spooked by a flapping length of yellow cloth caught in its bridle, bore down upon her.

Those spectators on the sidewalk who saw what was happening yelled a warning, but it was lost on her, since hooting and hollering was all part of the afternoon's celebration. Unaware of the danger, she remained in the middle of the street, changing her direction to walk toward Kinkade.

Waving frantically, Kinkade dashed toward her.

Puzzled by his overweening enthusiasm, she stopped in her tracks, directly in the path of the crazed animal.

Arms wide, Kinkade caught up to her.

Realizing his intention to grab her, she hung back.

Without a moment's hesitation Kinkade swept her into his arms.

Shocked, she struggled in his embrace, but his momentum thrust them out of the horse's path just as it thundered by, choking them with dust.

Apologizing profusely, Kinkade all but dropped her trying to prove he had meant no disrespect, when all he wanted to do most in the world was to hold her close.

Before she regained her balance, she realized he had saved her from a serious accident, perhaps death. "*Mahalo nui*, Mr. Kinkade," she murmured, wishing she could remain in the comfort of his embrace until her fright at the close call had abated.

Her desire showed clearly in her eyes, but Kinkade was too afraid he would never let her go if he touched her again. He took a step back to regain his composure as people began to gather around to congratulate him. The whooping and cheering had begun again, signaling the return of the riders. Even in the throes of his infatuation, wherein anything seemed possible, he knew it was beyond the bounds of acceptable behavior for anyone of his lowly position to ask for her permission to pay a formal call. Nonetheless, his heart would not allow him to pass up this golden opportunity. "May I see you again?" he asked hurriedly, being deliberately vague, and not a little breathless with his own daring.

Turning her attention to the now-teeming street, she waved at the large man galloping past, whose happy grin changed to a scowl when he spotted Kinkade so close to her.

"I shall ride in the park next Saturday, after the sun leaves mid-heaven," she said with a casual smile that set his heart racing. "Perhaps you would allow me to ride your beautiful horse?"

"I shall be there, with Crosspatches," Kinkade promised. Scarcely were the words out of his mouth when he was grabbed and smothered in a heartfelt hug from one of her well-rounded friends.

"Near the footbridge over the lily pond," she added when he was free of her friend's embrace. "Aloha!" And she was gone.

Those who had mounts regained them while, gathering the princess into their midst, the others resumed their positions as spectators.

Scarcely able to believe his good fortune, Kinkade was about to cross back over to the blacksmith when he remembered his engagement with Jacqueline. Knowing how much she was counting upon him, and that he was woefully late, he decided to settle his quarrel another day. Finding his bicycle, he leapt upon it and tore off for the hotel, happier than he had ever before been.

Red-faced with exertion, he arrived in a rush to be greeted by a furious Jacqueline.

"Where have you been?" she asked, near tears with frustration, her few precious free hours nearly spent.

Wasting no time, he set the brake on his bicycle and swiftly located the smallest cycle in the rack. Checking that there was no impending traffic in the huge courtyard, he held it steady and motioned for her to climb upon the seat. "I went to the horse parlor—that crook!"

Fear replaced anger as Jacqueline found herself stranded high on a perch, and the threat of toppling robbed her of her desire to scold.

"Now pedal!" Kinkade cried, holding on to the back of the seat to steady her.

Jacqueline froze. "I am falling!" The cycle wobbled dangerously.

"Trust me, Miss Bordeaux," Kinkade said gallantly, happily pretending that she was his Princess Lilliana. "I shall not allow you to fall." He gave her a slight shove while still holding on. "Now push!" he cried, trotting beside her.

Twice around the courtyard with Kinkade's careful tutelage, and, although still timid, Jacqueline felt steady enough to try an unassisted ride down the wide driveway—with Kinkade cycling close beside her. By the time they were halfway down the tree-shaded drive, her upset at his tardiness long forgotten, she felt secure enough to be able to talk while in motion. "I do not see you since we arrive, monsieur," she said, exhilarated by the speed. "Where do you keep yourself?"

Badly in need of advice, immensely grateful for the opening, Kinkade could contain himself no longer. From his first sight of the princess beside Crosspatches, to the promise of their tryst, he spilled his overflowing heart. Busy with her cycling, or so he thought, Jacqueline remained silent during his entire recital. "I must tell her the truth," he said at length. "But how?"

Jacqueline swerved to a stop. Standing astride the cycle, she waited for him to brake and turn to face her.

Much to Kinkade's amazement, she seemed angry.

"If you think I care the fig how you tell the princess you are the servant," she cried, somewhat out of breath from exercise and emotion, "you have the big mistake!"

Openmouthed, he stared after Jacqueline as she placed boot upon pedal, shoved off, and sped away with an expertise that left him wondering if her need for lessons had been a ruse.

The approach to the Tarkingtons' home was much like driving through a cool tunnel of every known shade of green. Shards of sunlight penetrated the dense overhang, providing just enough light to make carriage lamps unnecessary. Abigail found the gloom depressing and was greatly relieved when the drive opened up and the huge, tree-shaded white clapboard house, encircled by a lanai, loomed into view.

She and Maude were greeted on the steps by a silk-clad manservant in his distinctive Japanese pillbox cap who bowed them into a formal drawing room at the front of the house and bade them sit until Miss Tarkington could join them. When they were duly ensconced, Maude in the spool-backed straight chair near the window and Abigail in a chair much like it on the other side of a matching table, he offered them refreshments in his accented English. Both ladies chose iced tea, and he bowed himself out of the room, presumably to fetch it.

Abigail scarcely had time to arrange her skirts before Penelope swept into the room, hands outstretched in greeting. "I am so grateful that you have come, Miss Danforth." With a significant glance and inclusive nod in Maude's direction, she held Abigail's still-gloved hand a bit longer than etiquette required. "You are the answer to my prayers."

"Surely you overstate the case, Miss Tarkington," Abigail said, abashed by the lady's effusiveness.

Overriding Abigail's protest by ignoring it, Penelope took Maude's outstretched hand in both of hers and, patting it, continued, "What would you like? Lemonade? Papaya or mango juice perhaps?"

"Your man has already gone for tea, thank you," Maude replied, somewhat alarmed by Penelope's entrance. She knew full well how little tolerance Abigail had for the chatter of empty-headed women, and this was a very different lady who greeted them from the sober one she had met at the Daltons'.

"Has he now?" Penelope smiled as she settled her ample body on the settee facing him. "Well and good. Yasushi has been in our employ for only a few months. Still on trial, as it were, you know? He does seem to enjoy serving our guests, I must say."

"Then I am much impressed," Abigail responded, her voice flat.

Maude winced inwardly at her tone, recognizing the danger signal.

"Oh, I am pleased," Penelope continued, blissfully unaware of Abigail's prejudice. "Good, that is to say—honest—help is so hard to find . . . and keep. Hawaiians do tend to be so lazy, you know." She smiled at Abigail. "Or perhaps you don't, since you have been on the island such a short time."

Much to Maude's relief, before Abigail could reply, Yasushi returned bearing a tray laden with full glasses, an extra pitcher of iced tea, and plates heaped with delicacies. Placing the tray on the table in front of the settee, he put two napkins on the table between Abigail and Maude and placed their glasses of tea upon them. As he turned to the tray to serve Penelope her glass, she waved at him with a dismissive hand. "You may go, Yasushi."

He obeyed, bowing himself out of the room.

Ignoring the refreshments, before Penelope could comment, Abigail said, "What exactly do you wish me to do, Miss Tarkington?"

Penelope reached for her tea. "I must say, your directness is refreshing, Miss Danforth," she said with a sly wink at Maude. "Most people I know would consume an entire afternoon in idle conversation before getting to the point."

"I was given to understand that there was some urgency?" Abigail had noticed the wink, and struggled to mask her irritation. "Your father—?"

"It is not my father who is in danger, Miss Danforth." Penelope glanced at Maude with a puzzled expression.

"I told Miss Danforth about Matthew's predicament," Maude responded defensively.

"Did you tell her about Luke?" Taking a large swallow of tea, Penelope replaced her glass upon the table.

"Luke?" Maude's eyes widened with surprise as she glanced at Abigail, clearly indicating that she had never before heard the name.

"No, of course not, how foolish of me." Penelope glanced at the two women in turn. "How could you?" Pulling a lace hanky from her sleeve, she held it to her nose, sniffing her disapproval. "Everyone in this house pretends that he does not exist."

"Who is Luke, pray?" Abigail asked with growing impatience.

"My older brother by my father's first wife," Penelope responded. "Daddy disinherited him years ago. No one knows where he is." She lowered her voice to a whisper. "Father considers him dead." She shrugged. "He might very well be."

Maude glanced at Abigail, concerned that she was losing patience. Much to her surprise, Abigail leaned close to the obviously distraught woman with every show of sympathy.

"And you?" Abigail asked gently. Her own twin brothers were sworn enemies and, occasionally caught between them, their quarrels had caused her much difficulty. She understood Penelope's distress. Or thought she did. "What do you think?"

Penelope dabbed at her eyes as she spoke. "I believe that Luke is somehow poisoning Matthew."

Even though she felt she knew the answer, watching the large woman intently, Abigail asked, "And why would he do such a despicable thing to his own brother?"

Penelope looked at Abigail contemptuously, as if the answer should be obvious and not worth a response. "Matthew took his inheritance!"

"If you know your brother to be the villain, why do you require my services?"

"I do not know where Luke is!"

"But the police—?"

"I cannot tell the police!" she cried, horrified by the idea. "They would have to turn Matthew in at once, on pain of losing their jobs!"

Abigail sighed. She had not discussed the possibility with Maude, but the need to move in with the Tarkingtons seemed obvious. Hoping for an invitation, she said, "If indeed it is one brother against another, and if I am to protect the younger one from further harm, we should be nearby." She cast a fleeting glance at Maude.

Maude's silent shrug indicated that she had no objections if an invitation was forthcoming.

"I have only to tell Yasushi to have rooms prepared for you," Penelope said briskly. "You are more than welcome to move in at once."

The burning globe of sun was rapidly descending toward the sea as Princess Lilliana strolled along the shoreline, deep in thought. Crashing waves easily muffled the soundless step of bare feet on sand as the large man hurried toward her.

Startled, she smiled up at him when he reached her side, but when he tried to take her hand, she pulled away.

"No, William." She spoke softly.

"Oh for the day when I could invoke *kapu*!" he cried, jumping high in the air, shaking his fist at the sinking sun. He landed facing her, playfully blocking her path.

She looked up at him calmly, shaking her head, refusing his invitation to play. "What would you do, have me flogged?" she asked with a wry smile. "Or killed, perhaps?"

"I would stop you from chasing every haole you meet!"

"How can you be jealous of a horse?" She brushed past him.

He caught up to her easily. "It is the rider who—"

She stopped short and turned to look up at him again. The sun behind her cast her face in shadow. "Whatever was between us is over," she said, her voice firm.

"But why?" he cried, unable to conceal his anguish.

"I have changed my mind," she said, wishing she had the courage to tell him the truth.

"But you promised—"

"I shall do as I please," she said, her chin high. "You cannot stop me." Turning, she walked away.

William did not follow. He watched her figure shrink into the setting sun, absolutely certain he could win her back.

$\triangledown$

3

A LIGHT SPRINKLE DAMPENED Saturday's dawn in the park. Eels slithered beneath the lily pads, paying no attention to the fat, gold or freckled carp which, in turn, paid no notice to the myriad species of colorful gilled creatures that shared the universe of the pond. Some lazily vacuumed algae from the bottom while others energetically chased their prey, and still others nibbled for grubs on those roots that dangled near the surface in their common, incessant quest for food. Like finicky children, those that knew what precisely suited their diet ignored the body of Princess Lilliana. Those more adventuresome tried a bite.

Strewn with books, Abigail's rooms more nearly resembled a library than a boudoir with her gleanings from Honolulu's public and university libraries, and the not inconsiderable collection of books owned by the Tarkingtons. She had read the dry tomes on botany, toxicology, entomology, and ichthyology until her eyes ached, but had merely succeeded in getting muddled. Triggerfish, *muki-muki*, goatfish, and crown of thorn fish, et al., ad infinitum all swam in the Hawaiian waters, all were poisonous, but for only certain parts of the year. The list of toxic plants was endless, but while *Aconitum napellus* (monkshood) caused both tingling and numbness, it was so virulent that it was an unlikely choice, since a quick death did not seem to be the object in Matthew's case. *Mandragora officinarum* (mandrake) caused tingling, but it would also induce diarrhea and vomiting. And thus each possible potion had a disqualifying flaw, or was not easily obtained locally. Nor could she ask a resident scientist for guidance, since Matthew's symptoms would be immediately suspect.

Further, Matthew had been detained at the sugar mill, which had made questioning him impossible. It was only Penelope's importuning that had persuaded him to return today in time for tea, and an interview. His inaccessibility and apparent reluctance to see her had not improved her humor.

Her efforts to find Luke had stalled upon the necessity of waiting for the senior Tarkington to regain his strength. Thus frustrated at every turn, upon hearing a knock on her door, she all but shouted, "Come in!"

Kinkade entered and, softly closing the door behind him, crossed to the writing desk where Abigail was seated. "You rang, miss?"

"Oh, it is you." She glanced up briefly before returning her attention to her notes. "You need not exercise Crosspatches this afternoon."

"Oh, but I do not mind, miss," he said, devastated by the news. He'd been counting on riding the thoroughbred to the park to meet the princess, and tried to keep his disappointment from showing.

"I shall ride him after breakfast," she said, oblivious to his distress. "I am in much need of the exercise."

"Yes, miss." Having long been in service, he knew better than to insist. "Will there be anything else?"

Excused, Kinkade closed her door and slowly made his way down the back stairs. As he paused on the landing, for the first time in his life he considered deliberately disobeying orders. True, the horse might be tired if Abigail was in one of her moods to ride him hard, but there would be several hours to spare in which he could recoup. And once stabled, it was unlikely that Abigail would check. Had anyone else been so vague as to the time of their meeting, he'd have been annoyed, but he had been charmed by the princess's expression of the sun leaving the mid-heaven and, planning to reach the park at two, had been perfectly content at the prospect of waiting several hours, if need be. All the while Crosspatches could rest.

Energy generated by her outrage at Kinkade's folly served Jacqueline well through the packing and unpacking, the loading and unloading, the getting acquainted with the ins and outs of a new household during the days following her riding lesson. At least Abigail had lightened her burden by taking Maude as chaperon on her obsessive search for books.

But, tired as she was, sleep was hard to come by. Terrified by the stories of scorpions' and snakes' fondness for bedclothes, she would strip her cot and remake it, sometimes more than once, before climbing in. Once settled, Kinkade's adoring description of his princess—her hair, her eyes, her skin, her carriage, her smile, her bare feet—would hum in her brain like the mosquitoes outside the net buzzing to get at her. Had there been a headlamp on her new bicycle, a surprise gift from Abigail, which had irritated Maude into a stony three-day silence, she would have been tempted to go for a ride. Failing that, she lay awake planning her half-day's outing in light of her newfound freedom of movement. The park seemed the perfect destination. A footbridge should not be that difficult to find. And she could see for herself if the princess was as fair as Kinkade said.

Matthew held tight to his hairbrushes. Standing before the bureau mirror in his bedchamber, he vigorously applied them to the sides of his close-cropped, sun-streaked hair, closely calibrating the sensation he could perceive in the fingers of each hand—a habit he had formed since confessing his fears to his sister. His condition, which he preferred calling his collection of symptoms, had not deteriorated. Nor had it improved. Today, as most days, he had no difficulty holding the handleless brushes, although the tingling sensation in his right shin had returned after a week's absence. While the itch had responded to a salve that Penelope had provided, he found the unpredictability of the recurrence maddening. And frightening. Every schoolchild could recite the symptoms of the Chinese disease. Most agreed that a jump from Nuuana Pali was preferable.

Having just achieved his second decade, blessed with a tall, well-muscled physique, dancing gray eyes in a tanned, handsome face, wealth and gracious manners—there was not one maiden on the whole of Oahu, natives included, who would have denied him permission to call upon her. Busy learning the sugar industry, he spared himself little time to pay attention to the fair sex, but when he did, they invariably succumbed. He had stolen more than a few kisses, and had left more than one broken heart in his wake as a result. Both his father and Penelope had so often told him that he was a prize catch for some lucky damsel that he secretly believed them. But those gods who had smiled upon him so profusely had now decided to take it all away, he thought, and in an excruciatingly painful way at that. Swiftly, he amended his thoughts to capitalize God, and delete the s so that He became the one God, and a Methodist. No need to upset the old man, given his debilitated condition, even in his thoughts.

Grimacing at his silent wit in the mirror, he laid the brushes on their tray, whisked the shoulders of his well-fitting jacket, and straightened his cravat before declaring himself ready to meet the formidable Miss Danforth.

He was unused to rejection, and his condition had further undermined him. Even before his sister had talked out of turn, Abigail had made it clear that she despised him. She must be a perverse creature, indeed, if she was willing to see him now. How she might help him find out if he was being poisoned, and who was doing it if he was, when *he* did not know, was beyond his comprehension. Girls were for amusing oneself with. When one had the time.

Closing his bedchamber door, he hurried to the west-most lanai, which was *makai*, toward the sea, a favorite spot for tea since the sunsets could be spectacular. Looking even prettier than he remembered from their brief encounter at the Daltons', Abigail was seated primly in a rattan armchair rather than reclining on one of the *punees*. When he reached out his hand in greeting, she put hers in it willingly enough, but when he bent to kiss her fingertips, she pulled away.

"Sorry, I forgot," he said, blushing furiously. "You know my unclean secret."

"I beg your pardon?" she said, offended that he had taken advantage of her willingness to help him by indulging in an unwelcome romantic gesture.

He shrugged. "I do not blame you for being afraid that I might infect you," he said, ready to bolt at the first sign of her pity.

"I am not afraid!" Abigail exclaimed, insulted beyond measure. "Must I remind you that I am here to discover who is poisoning you?" Her tone was querulous as she reached for the pot to pour his tea. "We have no time to spare for dallying." Even as she reprimanded him, Abigail could not help but observe how singularly attractive the young man was. Her sympathies already engaged by her perilous position, she steeled herself against such errant thoughts. "One lump or two?" she asked, her voice flat, holding the tiny silver tongs aloft.

"None, thank you." Usually girls responded to his skillfully bestowed kiss and flirtatious expression with smiles. It was not uncommon for them to dissolve into fits of giggles, which rendered their eyes soft and inviting. Not so Abigail. He pulled up a matching rattan chair at an angle to the table that held the tea service. Seating himself, he nodded his thanks for the tea, took a sip, and bided his time.

"I must ask you some questions, Mr. Tarkington." Hoping

to put him at ease, she did not look at him directly, but gave her entire attention to the task of stirring a spoonful of sugar into her tea as she continued. "Given the nature of your— ah—difficulty, you may find them personal, if not indelicate."

"Fire away, Miss Danforth," he replied in that overhearty manner used with children. "My sister warned me that you fancy yourself to be a consulting detective."

"It is no mere fancy, Mr. Tarkington," she replied, unruffled by his taunting demeanor. He was not the first man, nor was he likely to be the last, who had difficulty taking her seriously.

"You must admit it is a queer profession for a girl." Leaning forward, Matthew placed his cup on the table. "Especially one as pretty as you," he added with a teasing grin.

Abigail drew herself tall, her expression grim. "We are not here to discuss my appearance, Mr. Tarkington—"

"I daresay, Miss Danforth," he interrupted. "But beauty is its own excuse for being."

Abigail bristled. "Nor am I here to listen to quotes from Emerson, sir," she replied, her voice ice.

Matthew was unaware that he had quoted anyone, knowing only that the compliment had pleased every girl he'd ever said it to, but before he could find a reply, a bone-deep pain shot through his right shin. He gasped, all color draining from his face.

Alarmed by his obvious distress, all resentment at this patronizing behavior disappeared. "Are you all right, Mr. Tarkington?"

"It is nothing," he lied. The pain subsided as quickly as it had come, but it left him badly shaken. He knew only too well that he had just received a clear signal that the disease was progressing. "Do you really believe someone might be trying to poison me?" His shin ached with the memory, and he could not hide the fear that clouded his eyes.

"I shall endeavor to find out," she replied with a confidence she was far from feeling, since her research had proven so hollow. "Do you feel well enough to answer some questions?"

"Of course!" he snapped, offended that she might think him so weak that a little pain could deter him.

"Would you happen to know the whereabouts of your brother?"

"My brother?" Matthew looked blank for a moment. "Ahhhh!" he exhaled. "You must be referring to the Tarkington skeleton." His laugh was harsh. "Luke is twenty years older than I, Miss Danforth. If I saw him once, I do not remember it. And should I meet him on the street, it is unlikely I should recognize him."

"I see," she said thoughtfully, filing away his response and its fleeting revelation of bitterness. "Might I ask when you first noticed your symptoms?"

It took all his self-control to refrain from rubbing his shin, and it cost him his good temper. "You are one for questions, are you not?" His tone was irritable.

"It should be obvious to you that I must make inquiries if I am to find answers, sir," she said, beginning to lose patience. With a great effort at regaining it, she continued reasonably, "It would be most helpful if I knew when your— ah—difficulties began."

He shrugged. "I do not remember."

"Come, come, Mr. Tarkington." She glanced at him in disbelief. "You cannot remember such an important event?"

"My life is an active one, Miss Danforth," he said impatiently, yet with an appraising glance at the serious girl. Even as he spoke, he wondered if a smile would soften her expression and make her more feminine. "I ride the fields with the *luna*, and work with the men in the mill. When the waves are up, and I have time, I surf. If I gave note to every bump and scrape, I'd soon be branded a hypochondriac—or worse."

"Then I do not suppose you would recall a bite from an insect of some kind—?"

He laughed outright. It was not a merry sound. "Have you

not suffered through an invasion of our infamous mosquitoes?" he asked scornfully.

Abigail blushed, furious with herself for not thinking the question through.

His grin was mischievous as he leaned forward to speak in a conspiratorial tone. "Why, there are swarms of centipedes in the piles of bagasse right outside my office. Enough to give an army symptoms. I might have been bitten at any time."

Abigail closed her eyes. "An articulated arthropod animal of the class Myriapoda and order Chilopoda, because of its many legs. Most are harmless. Those of the genus *Scolopendra* do attain great size." There was a slight twinkle in her eyes when she opened them. "While the larger ones are poisonous, you would most certainly have a large welt at the site, and probably run a fever." Her smile was fleeting, and did nothing to soften her expression. "Not a likely culprit, sir."

Her recitation appalled him. "Is that so?" he replied, his eyes wide. "Now what on earth would possess a girl to fill her pretty little head with all that nonsense?"

Abigail had much on her mind to accomplish in the short time they were allowed to be alone together, and did not wish to be distracted from her goal. But his reaction so annoyed her that she could not resist responding, "To save you from Molokai, sir!"

He stood and paced to the edge of the lanai before returning to stand over her. "And what makes you think you can do that?"

Abigail looked directly into his eyes. "I can but try, Mr. Tarkington."

"My meddlesome sister had no business talking to you!" Suddenly he bent down and, placing his hands on the arms of her chair, bent alarmingly close to her face. "It is against nature for girls to spout science, and ask so many questions." Raising himself up, he bowed slightly. "Now, if you will excuse me, I must look in on Father." Turning on his heel, he left a nonplussed Abigail staring after him.

* * *

Dressed in Mr. Danforth's Saville Row castaways, complete with scarcely worn, fine leather riding gloves, Kinkade looked the part of the comfortable gentleman as he took care to ride Crosspatches slowly, which was actually trying for both of them, since the great horse liked nothing better than to run straight out. The opportunity to satisfy Princess Lilliana's desire for a ride, and thereby the perfect excuse for seeing her again, far outweighed any misgivings he might have had for his misdemeanor. Nor had he examined his motives in dressing himself as if he belonged to the leisure class. It did not occur to him to worry that some of those people he passed en route to the park who had stared at him, and his mount, so admiringly, might speak of the sight to someone in the closely knit social circle of Honolulu that included the Tarkingtons, and who in turn might mention the well-dressed stranger on the superb mount to Abigail.

High clouds crossed overhead, blown too swiftly by the trades to release any moisture. Dismounting, even he, who had little appreciation for nature, having spent most of his life in indoor pursuits, was taken with the beauty of the day. The park was an idyllic setting in which to meet a fairy princess. While it was far from crowded, he was not alone, yet he felt that Crosspatches would be safe tethered to a banyan tree within sight, and as he strolled toward the footbridge, he actually began to enjoy the view.

All week long he had seen the princess's face wherever he looked. All he had to do now was gaze down the path and he could imagine that it was she strolling toward him beneath the dainty parasol, dressed like a haole wahine to please him. Or she might arrive upon a horse, so he looked around at every sound of hoofbeats. And even as he placed his elbows upon the handrail near the far shore to gaze into the pond, he could imagine he saw her face. Time evaporated as he stood mesmerized by the flickering tails of color weaving in and out of the miniature islands formed by the lilies. They could be the flowered cloth of the garments she favored.

He could even imagine that he saw her face in the depths. And in time, he did. Utterly unaware that any sound escaped his lips, he screamed.

With no spare time to make friends with the cook, Jacqueline promised to mend a tear in the pocket of his best jacket in trade for a piece of his succulent fried chicken and a chunk of bread for her picnic. That and a blanket packed in the basket between the handlebars had at first made the bicycle difficult to steer, but she soon got the hang of it.

Upon reaching the park, she easily found the footbridge, and many trees to choose from to conceal herself while keeping it in view.

Her outrage knew no bounds when Kinkade eventually rode into view, mounted on Abigail's horse like it belonged to him, spiffed up like the gentleman. He even walked differently, all puffed out like he owned the bridge. When at length it appeared that he would remain at his post, staring into the pond, she unfolded the napkin containing her lunch. She had just finished the last bite of chicken, and was cleaning her fingers, when she heard his cry.

Shocked by the heartbroken sound, she watched him plunge into the pond, thrash around among the lily pads and, moaning with effort, pull what looked like a bundle of clothes from the water, and drag it to shore. Before her horrified eyes, he turned and was violently sick into the pond. And then she saw the bare feet. Two men ran up to help, and soon the crowd around Kinkade and his burden was so thick that she could no longer see him.

Stunned, trying to decide what to do, she watched the scene unfold as the police arrived. She ached to go to him. But he would hate her if he knew she had spied on him. And with all the people surrounding him, he did not need her.

Slowly, tears making it difficult to see, she folded her blanket and restored it to the basket. Holding the bicycle by the handlebars, stopping every few yards to mop her eyes with a handkerchief, she began the long journey back to the Tarkingtons'.

*   *   *

Yasushi had cleared tea from the *makai* lanai and been dismissed by his mistress. Lingering by the doorway, he tried to hear what the ladies were discussing. After the young master had stormed off to see his father, Miss Danforth had summoned his mistress and had also requested the pleasure of Miss Cunningham's presence. The young master's name seemed to dominate their conversation, but the telephone rang and he was forced to leave his post.

"Yes, Miss Danforth stays with us," he continued after answering as he'd been taught. "The police?" he repeated, glancing at the receiver. Never before had the officials called at the house, and it unnerved him. "I tell her you wish to speak to her." With all due speed he placed the receiver upon the hall table and hurried to the lanai.

Curious upon hearing the nature of the call, Penelope accompanied Abigail to the telephone. Yasushi hid himself behind the door in the parlor, within earshot.

"I am Miss Danforth," Abigail said, pausing to listen. "Yes, yes, Kinkade is staying here." She paused again. "No, no, he is not my relative, he is in my employ," she responded. "I am quite sure!" she replied huffily. "Has anything untoward happened to him?"

"No, ma'am," the police officer said, his voice as clear as if he were in the room. "But he has been involved in a serious incident."

"But you just said he was all right!"

"No, ma'am, the incident was not to him," the officer replied. "That is, he was not the one who was drowned."

"Pray explain yourself!" Abigail said. Hand over the mouthpiece, she turned to Penelope. "There has been an accident," she said in a rush. "Someone drowned."

Returning her attention to the telephone, Abigail did not see Penelope's alarmed expression.

"Well, this Kinkade fellow found her, you see?" the officer continued.

"Found who?" Abigail asked.

"Princess Lilliana."

Abigail repeated the name to Penelope before speaking again into the phone. "I do not understand the reason for this call, Officer."

Feeling faint, Penelope sank into the chair by the small table that held the telephone.

"We are detaining him, miss," the officer explained. "I thought you might want to come and see him."

"Detaining him!" Abigail exclaimed, concerned about her hostess, who had suddenly turned pale. "How dare you? You must release him at once!"

"I am afraid that is impossible, miss," the officer replied.

"And why might that be, pray?" Abigail asked in her most imperious manner.

The officer paused before continuing with a weary sigh. "Mr. Kinkade has confessed to murder."

$\triangledown$

4

A BASTION OF CIVILIZATION amid the uncivil devastation, the police station stood unharmed on the corner of Merchant and Bethel streets, so near the edge of what was left of Chinatown after the burning that the smell of char still hung in the air despite months of cleansing ocean breezes. Word of a drowning spread faster than the horses pulling the police van could make their way from the park to the stationhouse. Along with the curious who had tagged along after the wagon, a small group of idle stevedores and seamen with time to kill strolled up from the wharves, shots of cheap whiskey under their belts. They milled about outside seeking some relief from the tedium of life ashore, mingling with those Hawaiians who had gathered upon hearing that the victim was one of their own.

In the interest of speed, rather than wait for the Tarkingtons' phaeton to be horsed, Abigail ordered Crosspatches saddled.

Having been handsomely paid by Kinkade not to tattle, the stableboys volunteered to hitch the carriage in a jiffy instead.

When, through Penelope, Abigail insisted upon riding her

horse, they admitted that it was missing, but claimed not to know who had taken it.

Matthew had also disappeared, but it was soon ascertained that he had ridden off upon his own horse.

With Penelope shrieking that they would all be fired, Abigail declared that she would wait and report the missing horse when they reached the police station, while Maude volunteered to stay behind to set about discovering its whereabouts.

Still upset by Matthew's rejection, Abigail had hoped to continue her interrupted conversation with Penelope in the carriage, but that good lady had decided to drive, leaving the driver behind to answer to Maude. Had she known Penelope's penchant for speed, Abigail would have realized that conversation would be impossible when Penelope, hat askew, had reins in her hands. Further, she would have insisted upon questioning the driver herself to free him for the task. By the time they pulled up in front of the stationhouse, Abigail was clinging to the side of the carriage for dear life with one hand, and holding her hat to her head with the other. A small crowd of onlookers, eager for some distraction, had gathered. Finding no place to park in front, Penelope was forced to drive halfway down the block before they could descend from the phaeton and make their way into the station. The detour took them in the opposite direction from where Crosspatches was hitched, so that neither lady was aware of his presence.

It was not often that the precinct entertained ladies of Miss Tarkington's social standing, and upon introducing themselves at the front desk, they were immediately squired into the absent captain's private office, where they were made comfortable in straight chairs pulled around his desk in anticipation of their arrival.

While drownings were not uncommon, most bodies were washed ashore from the ocean, not pulled from a shallow lily pond; nor was the body of a dead princess often stored in the morgue. A self-confessed gentleman murderer, who might not be a gentleman after all, was also rare. All in all, the uniformed officers on duty were having an unusual Saturday afternoon, and although the captain's office was supposed to be more private than most, lots had been cast and the winning officer, one Drew Miller, was posted inside with the ladies. Every other man on duty found reason to look in, if only to feign suddenly realizing that the captain was not present.

Their swift removal to the haven of privacy had precluded Abigail's mentioning her missing horse, but as soon as they were seated, tucking the last tendrils of windblown hair into place, she turned to Officer Miller, whose mustache seemed larger than he. "I wonder if I might trouble you to report that my horse is missing?" She managed a smile even while straightening her skirts.

In a trice, Miller summoned another officer, whose mustache, while large, was more suited to his face. He took the information down in such a competent manner that he was opening the door to leave just as Kinkade was ushered in, hands cuffed in front, accompanied by two more uniformed officers, one clean-shaven.

"What are you doing in Father's clothes!" Abigail exclaimed before he could be seated.

"He gave them to me, Miss Danforth," Kinkade replied with a lift to his chin to salvage his pride. "I thought it fitting to wear my best when meeting a princess."

Abigail was dumbfounded that a servant of hers would dare approach royalty except on some errand for her. "What did you think you were doing," she waved her hand about, trying to find words, "meeting this—this princess?"

"Princess!" Penelope exclaimed. "She is no more princess than I." Her round cheeks pink with indignation, she continued, "Who told you she was royalty?"

"Princess Lilliana herself," Kinkade replied with great dignity, numbed by the pain of her loss.

"Ridiculous pretensions!" Penelope fanned herself violently. "She was born on the wrong side of the blanket, like most of those heathens."

Abigail blushed. "Out of wedlock?"

Standing about as though they had been suddenly transported into someone's best parlor rather than secure in their place of work, the three police officers exchanged amazed glances that society ladies would speak of such things.

"Sisters even mate with brothers!" Penelope replied with disgust. "They multiply like fleas."

"Princess Lilliana is—was—no heathen," Kinkade replied defiantly. "She was the most beautiful girl I have ever met."

Abigail could scarcely believe his effrontery, but however well warranted, it would not do to dress him down in front of strangers. Resolving to have it out with him in private, she smiled coolly at the clean-shaven officer. "Pray, remove the handcuffs, sir."

"I am afraid I cannot do that, miss," he replied.

His mustachioed companion, who had been first to arrive on the scene, added, "He found the body, miss."

"And is it your custom to restrain everyone who discovers a corpse?" Abigail asked indignantly.

"No, ma'am," he replied.

"He confessed to murder," the clean-shaven one added before turning his head to listen to the racket, which was rapidly increasing outside the door.

"You cannot possibly believe that he would do such a thing!" she exclaimed indignantly. "Just look at him," she added, although she realized she did not have the officer's full attention. "Does he look like a murderer to you?" Even as she spoke, she realized how ridiculous she sounded. She, more than any other person in the room, knew that one could not detect a killer from his appearance. Indeed, if such a feat were possible, there would be no need for her chosen profession.

The clean-shaven officer had his mouth open to respond when the door burst open and an enormous Hawaiian, face livid with paint, filled the doorway. "Where is he?" he bellowed.

Penelope screamed.

Abigail gasped, placing a hand to her bosom to still her beating heart.

Kinkade stood so swiftly, his chair crashed to the floor.

Officer Miller, hands outstretched in a gesture of peace, dashed over to place himself between the large, angry native and Kinkade.

Kinkade's escorts were at William's sides and had grabbed his arms before he could raise them. "He killed her!" William cried, scowling at Kinkade. "Let me at him!"

The two officers held on tight, and managed to confine him to the doorway while Kinkade backed away behind the captain's desk.

"We do not know that he did it," Officer Miller said soothingly.

With subtle nods of the head, the two officers signaled to Miller that they had detected the smell of alcohol. Noted for their easygoing dispositions, native Hawaiians had no tolerance for liquor. From bitter experience, the officers knew it could easily take ten men to quell a man of William's size who was contaminated with drink. Their best recourse was to ease him from the scene and, if possible, out of the station-house.

"But I saw them together," William cried, shaking off his captors' arms with ease. Noting that he was no longer trying to rush the room, they willingly released him. "Haole pig had no business talking to her."

Miller gestured toward Kinkade. "You can see we have him handcuffed."

Kinkade held his cuffed arms aloft so that William could see.

"I assure you we will conduct a complete investigation," Miller continued.

Penelope found her voice. "How do you know she did not commit suicide?" she cried.

"Miss Tarkington!" Miller exclaimed, wishing he could throttle her.

"She would never commit suicide!" William's voice filled

the room. "Someone had to hold her under." He glared at Kinkade.

Abigail was appalled by the obvious hatred that passed between the two men.

"We do not know that yet," the officer who was first on the scene replied. "There were no marks of violence on her body." He shuddered inwardly at the memory of what the fish had done.

The two officers stepped away as Miller approached, a sympathetic hand outstretched. "Her death is a tragedy, to be sure." His voice was soothing as he stretched his arm to place it around the large Hawaiian's shoulders and gently turn him from the room. "You can see that we are doing all we can to find out who killed her."

William turned to point an accusing finger at Kinkade. "You will keep him in jail?"

Willing to tell the man anything to get him to leave peacefully, Miller responded sincerely, "He will not leave our custody until the killer is found."

Those men who had gathered near the captain's door in case reinforcements were needed casually dispersed, but remained nearby watching the Hawaiian's every move as Miller, speaking softly, escorted him to the front door.

As soon as Miller had talked the large man out of the captain's room, the clean-shaven officer shut the door and, briefly resting his back against it, heaved a sigh of relief.

"Lazy no-good sinner." Penelope leaned close to Abigail so that only she could hear as she whispered behind her fan. "Unrepentant alcoholics, the lot of them."

Abigail thought it an uncharitable opinion for a missionary's daughter, but made no reply.

A much-relieved Kinkade returned to his chair as the mustachioed officer restored it to its upright position.

Miller had his hand on the doorknob, about to rejoin them, when he heard his name being called. Hoping it was not the angry William returned, he looked over his shoulder. The officer who had taken the information about Crosspatches caught up with him. "You will not believe where I found Miss Danforth's horse, sir," he said breathlessly.

"Well?"

"Hitched to the patrol wagon."

"Are you sure?" Miller's huge mustache hid his smile.

The officer nodded eagerly. "It is a thoroughbred all right, and it's got that white patch that looks like a big *x* on its nose!"

Thinking it the best possible news, Miller announced the officer's findings as soon as he entered the room and had closed the door on his curious fellow officers.

Kinkade stared at his cuffed hands. He could only hope that Abigail would not give him the boot in front of a roomful of strangers.

"What were you doing, riding my horse after I expressly told you not to?" Abigail glared at him.

"I thought—"

"What were you trying to do?" she demanded. "Fob yourself off as a gentleman?"

"No, ma'am," he replied with the utmost dignity. "I did not want to shame the Danforth name. I wanted to make a good impression."

"This has gone on long enough." Eager to get Kinkade alone where she could tell him her thoughts, Abigail addressed Officer Miller in her most imperious tones. "Release him at once to my care."

"But he has confessed—"

Abigail turned to Kinkade. "Retract your statement this minute!"

Kinkade shook his head stubbornly. "I cannot do that, miss," he said, his mouth set.

"He might be safer in jail, what with that loony Hawaiian after him," Penelope muttered.

Kinkade cleared his throat. "Will you investigate, Miss Danforth?"

"I should say not!" Abigail exclaimed. "The police are perfectly capable of finding the killer, if there was one."

"Then I killed her," Kinkade said.

"That is preposterous!" Abigail exclaimed.

"It might have been an accident," the officer who had been first on the scene responded.

"How can you be so sure?" Kinkade asked.

The officer shrugged. "The postmortem examination will shed more light upon the matter in which she met her death."

"How soon can you perform the examination?" Abigail asked.

"Tomorrow is Sunday—" Miller shrugged.

"And you must detain him?"

"He has confessed to murder, Miss Danforth."

"Very well!" As Abigail stood, so did Kinkade.

Penelope gained her feet, and all the officers straightened themselves, the young clean-shaven one adjusting his tie.

"Perhaps it is for the best." Abigail walked over to Kinkade and raked him with a furious glance. "You wear my father's clothes," she said. "You ride my horse against my wishes!" Turning her back on him, her petticoats rustled angrily as she headed for the door. "For all I care, you can rot in jail!"

Jacqueline despaired of ever falling asleep. Scorpions and snakes were the least of her worries. Maude had been in a perfect pet when she had arrived back at the Tarkingtons', questioning everyone, including Yasushi, who could clearly know nothing since his duties were restricted to the house, regarding the whereabouts of Crosspatches. She had been forced to commit the venial sin of lying that she knew nothing, since by revealing that she knew the truth she would betray herself as well as Kinkade. Her guilt knew no bounds.

Eaten alive with worry upon discovering that Abigail and Penelope had been summoned to the police station, she had been so distraught when they returned without Kinkade that she could not touch her dinner, which had insulted the cook so badly that she feared she'd lost the only friend she'd begun to make in the household, since he had much admired the mending she had done.

Never before had she seen her mistress so upset. Abigail had not uttered a word during their entire bedtime ritual, nor had Jacqueline had the temerity to interrupt her thoughts, or so much as mention Kinkade's name.

A grim-faced Maude had knocked upon the door just as Jacqueline had finished braiding Abigail's hair, and she had gratefully fled the room upon being excused. As pests go, the mosquitoes were no worse than her own questions of whom to tell what she had seen of what Kinkade had done. If anyone. And what, exactly, come to think of it, had she seen?

It was a bad night for mosquitoes. Before Jacqueline had closed the door behind her, Abigail rose from the dressing table. Depositing her dressing gown on the back of the chair, she beckoned for Maude, who kept hers on, to join her and, although floor-length nightgowns protected them from neck to wrist, the two ladies dashed under the netting that surrounded her large bed. "You must book passage on the first available ship sailing stateside," Abigail said, propping herself up on pillows.

"But what of Kinkade?" Maude asked, arranging herself cross-limbed at the foot of the bed, facing Abigail. "You cannot mean to leave him behind—in jail!"

"The police will set him free as soon as he recants." Abigail did not doubt her words. "Let him cool his heels in a locked cell until Monday. And eat prison food."

"What if he sticks by his story?"

"Impossible!" Abigail exclaimed "You will see!" Abigail shook her head in wonderment. "I cannot imagine what possessed him to try and fob himself off as a gentleman."

"She cannot imagine?" Maude gazed heavenward, then looked directly at Abigail. "Oh, great observant one?"

"Well, what is it?" Abigail asked querulously. "Speak up!"

Maude shrugged. "That which you have forsworn, and therefore may be excused for being blind to."

"Emotion?" Abigail asked, genuinely puzzled.

"No mere emotion, my dear Miss Danforth." Maude

sighed heavily. "Cupid's arrow struck a true blow."

"Are you trying to say that Kinkade was in love with that—that—princess?"

"What else would turn him into such a blathering idiot that he would confess to a crime he did not commit?"

"But how?" Abigail was amazed. "How could he possibly have had time to court her? Did he not know that his situation was impossible?"

Maude nodded in agreement. She paused before continuing, her voice hollow with longing. "But I daresay he would not trade places with anyone."

"Do not dare quote Tennyson!" Abigail exclaimed, clapping her hands over her ears. "If you speak of a young man's fancy in spring, I shall scream." She removed her hands. "I have endured quite enough Emerson from Mr. Tarkington."

"He made the capital mistake of commenting upon your beauty, did he?" Maude bit her lip to keep from smiling.

"You might have warned me that he is a condescending bore!"

"Come, come, Miss Danforth," Maude said soothingly. "Mr. Tarkington's attitude does not really surprise you, does it?"

Abigail groaned.

"You know perfectly well that it disturbs most men for a woman to exercise her brain beyond entertaining him upon the piano, or singing. There is no need to get overwrought."

Maude was right, but still his rejection of who she was rankled.

"Miss Tarkington will be most distressed by your desire to leave so precipitously."

"It seems pointless to remain." Abigail sighed. "Her brother has most emphatically refused my help. Who am I to say him nay?"

"And you seriously intend to abandon Kinkade in jail?"

Abigail folded her arms across her chest. "Who am I to interfere with people's lives?"

"What if he writes to your father!" Maude exclaimed. "Then what?"

Face stern, arms still folded, Abigail glared at her.

Maude drew a finger across her throat. "End of your career."

"Some reputation as a detective I am accumulating!" Abigail said bitterly. "Solving crimes for my relatives—and servants!"

"Miss Danforth!" Maude exclaimed, deeply offended by Abigail's implication that she had been an unworthy client because they were distantly related.

Abigail's eyes grew black with anger. "I wonder if I might ask you to excuse me, Miss Cunningham," she said, her voice cold. "It has been a long day."

Mouth set in a stern line, Maude refrained from further comment, except for a curt observance of bedtime etiquette. Anxious to quit Abigail before a quarrel ensued that might not be repaired, she wasted no time finding her slippers and dashing out of the room to the sanctuary of her own mosquito netting.

Abigail smacked the pillows much harder than necessary. "To think I have come to this!" she muttered. "Blackmailed by my own servant!"

Like breath from the gods, the breeze tried to blow out the torches held by the circle of mourners in the moonless night. Their voices chanting prayers from time beyond memory blended with the restless ocean. And thus, in a secret spot, known only to those privileged few, a vigil for the soul of the dead princess was kept.

▽

5

Dawn, with its promise of another empty day, was the worst time for Abner Tarkington. The brighter his room became, the darker his mood. Especially on the Sabbath. A vigorous man in his youth, he was unaccustomed to indulging in the deadly sin of sloth, and had vociferously held forth against it in many a sermon. For him, sleep had been incidental. Bed had always meant the delights of a female body to fondle, a personal idiosyncrasy that he neglected to share with his congregation. Now his bed was a prison. Forced to lie in it day in and day out, bereft of female companionship, his memories brought him only torment.

He had just turned nineteen, a tall, broad-chested, wide-shouldered man with lively blue eyes and a much-practiced, irresistible grin, when he married his first wife. His desire for the fragile blond girl with the sky-blue eyes and sweet lips made for kissing had become so overwhelming, he had risked his final year's grades at the seminary to claim her. Although his grades dropped alarmingly, he scraped by, happier than he had ever known he could be. Obsessed with her body, and his own pleasure, he failed to notice that his wife, soon pregnant, did not share his ardor.

In the spring of 1860, the infant Luke shared their voyage

to his mission on Oahu. That winter, pregnant again, his wife had passed too close to the open hearth while preparing their evening meal, setting fire to her skirts. A not uncommon occurrence. But she had taken an uncommonly long time to die. She had begged him to hasten her passing, and witnessing her agony had put his faith to the test. But he had persevered and convinced her to wait for the Lord to take her to His bosom in His own time. Their stillborn child had been another son. At her funeral, he had handed over the screaming one-year-old Luke to a converted, childless Hawaiian family to raise.

Although the lusty young minister did not lack for consolation among his congregants, his robust nature drove him to seek outlets beyond his ministry. Against the advice of the elders, he remained single, his reputation tainted by gossip, until his involvement in sugarcane forced him to give up the ministry altogether so that he could apply himself full-time to becoming rich. Since his personal ambition coincided so obviously with the best interests of the islands, he was blissfully unaware of having made a choice between God and Mammon.

It was a backbreaking struggle for twelve years, until the beautiful, wealthy Miss Margaret Slocum arrived from the mainland to visit relatives for a holiday. She refused his importuning outright, forcing him into the bonds of matrimony, a not altogether disagreeable arrangement for him.

He built her a large house and installed servants so that she need never go near a kitchen fire. To no avail. She died giving birth to Penelope. Shortly after, in 1875, the passage of the Reciprocity Act exempted sugar from import duty, giving increased political power to the small group of American planters to which he belonged. With his wife's inheritance, he imported cheap labor from all over the world. And worked harder than ever.

By the time Luke verged upon manhood, he was a stranger. Abner found him distant and belligerent, with the unforgivable arrogance to disagree with him about everything. Unable to control his son, he banished him to the mainland to school.

Determined not to lose his second child, he took Penelope everywhere with him. Before she could walk, she was riding in front of him as he surveyed his holdings with the *luna*.

The wealthy, handsome bachelor and doting father had little difficulty satisfying his carnal nature. His position in sugar assured his position in society. Thus secure, he discovered a fondness for the intrigue necessary to cuckold his friends. His growing reputation as a roué merely served to titillate the ladies. Knowing his sad history, before he even approached her, each thought she could be the one who could console, and thereby tame, him. All paid a great deal of attention to Penelope.

Shortly after Penelope's sixth birthday, celebrated with much fanfare, Mrs. Gwendolyn Abrams became pregnant. Married to Mr. Abrams, who had survived the Civil War a hero but rendered sterile by a stray bullet, the scandal of her condition rocked Honolulu. The heartbroken Mr. Abrams would have gladly kept his young wife and her issue, only too happy to have an heir, but Gwendolyn preferred the more exciting Abner. They were married three days before Matthew entered the world. With the passage of but a few days, Penelope had a new mother and a baby brother competing for her father's time. She did not fare well.

Nor did Gwendolyn. Resentful that he'd been forced to give her his name, Abner withheld all else. Mr. Abrams had put a bullet through his head on her wedding day and, blaming her, even those best friends who had stuck by her thus far, cut her. Seeing her only as a rival for her father, Penelope openly spurned her. With no one to turn to, Gwendolyn turned to drink. In less than a year the alcohol and cocaine had so debilitated her that she had no strength to outrun the incoming tide, and was swept from the outcropping of rock where it was her habit to go for solace. Sent to look for her stepmother who was late for dinner, it was Penelope who had discovered her lifeless body.

Because he had done the right thing by her, Abner's reputation survived Gwendolyn's death, which was termed a tragic accident, there being no apparent motive for suicide. Thrice widowed, he turned his full attention to his new son. Like Penelope, he had the boy sharing his saddle before he could walk. At first, Penelope followed them on her own horse, to take charge of the infant when it was necessary for her father to stop and discuss some problem with the *luna*. But she proved inept at mothering, allowing Matthew to toddle off too far into the cane, so even during those months when school was not in session, he hired tutors to keep her busy.

Having learned his lesson with Gwendolyn, he had confined his attentions to those married ladies who had produced children. One such alliance had lasted for a decade without discovery, only recently ending upon the woman's return to California with her ailing husband. He had missed her more than he thought possible. Shortly after her departure, he'd had his first heart attack. And now his heart ached in earnest as yet another empty day began, and he waited for Penelope to bring his breakfast.

Dawn's light found Abigail emerging from the Tarkingtons' stables astride Crosspatches. Although she had duly noted the cascades of purple and magenta blossoms plunging from steep rock, the hedges of green speckled with huge red flowers that framed bungalows set deep in shade, and graceful palms swaying against an ever-changing sky, it was not the beauty of the island that charmed her, but the custom of wahines riding astride. She no longer felt an outcast as she urged her horse to the gallop.

Finding the footbridge once she'd reached the park was simple. The sun having risen, more simple still was finding the spot where the princess's body had been dragged ashore; wheel tracks from the police van clearly marked the way. Dismounting, she dropped the reins in a bush and, crossing the footbridge, found the prints of Crosspatches's hooves where Kinkade said they would be. As she recrossed the bridge, she paused upon reaching the center to see what kind of privacy a killer might have were he to have drowned her on the spot.

She concluded that it was unlikely that the deed had been done by holding her under water. The pond was in easy view from many spots on the footpath, and she surely would have thrashed about trying to save herself. But banyan trees abounded, and many shadowy places existed in their tangled trunks to provide the privacy for a strangling, or knifing. The constant squawking of ducks might mask a scream. It would then be a relatively simple matter to wait until the coast was clear to drop her body in, letting the lily pads do the rest.

As she gazed into the pond, she was impressed that Kinkade had found her at all, so thick were the lilies. All hope that her death had been an accident vanished. Perhaps had she turned her back on the ocean, and been found on a sandy beach, but in a lily pond? Even had she jumped from the bridge, the water was shallow enough to stand in unless she'd been injured beforehand, and it would have taken an inhumanely dedicated effort to hold oneself under.

Until that moment she had believed Kinkade's discovering the body to have been a coincidence. But now she wondered if the killer had known that Kinkade would be meeting the princess. But who had known he would be there? He had found it easy enough to keep his tryst a secret, she thought indignantly. He had even found it a simple matter to use her horse without her knowledge.

Before her temper could rise again, she quit the bridge. Questions whirled in her head as she lifted her skirts to keep them from trailing in the mud as she walked along the shore looking for signs of a scuffle. Aware even as she did so that she might be trampling on the very spot where the princess had been thrown in, she peered for footprints. As in the case of the tracks by the police van and horses, there was too much evidence. Too many people, children and adults alike, had come to the edge to feed the ducks, and all had left prints, ducks included, along with a goodly supply of their feathers and droppings. Nor could she discern the age of the prints.

As she mounted Crosspatches, she had many questions to ask Kinkade, but she decided to head back to the Tarkingtons' for breakfast instead. The least she could do was make him sweat it out until Monday.

Sunday breakfast was a casual affair at the Tarkingtons'—fruit, the ever-present poi, muffins and coffee from the buffet—and not indulged in at all if Communion was in the offing. With church services as the ultimate destination, members of the household and guests were expected to appear in various stages of readiness to partake in just enough sustenance to survive until the large meal for lunch. It had become Penelope's habit to fix her father's tray from the buffet on Sundays, and she was thus occupied with selecting chunks of pineapple when Matthew appeared in the doorway.

Matthew had managed to avoid his sister since his interview with Abigail. Hoping she had not seen him, since her attention was on the buffet, he decided to leave rather than confront her now. Too late.

Spotting her brother in the doorway, Penelope's face blotched with anger. "You ungrateful brat!" she cried, shaking the serving fork at him. "I suppose you prefer to jump from Nuuanu Pali."

His face clouded with anger. "When will you stop meddling in my life?"

"I was just trying to help—"

"Like hell you were—"

"I will not have you blaspheming in this house!" Penelope cried, outraged. "Especially on the Sabbath!"

Matthew turned on his heel and left.

"If Father heard you it would be the death of him!" she muttered, jabbing a slice of papaya.

"Who is there?" Startled from a doze he did not care to admit he had relaxed into, Abner's voice had an edge of anger, which he used to disguise his drowsiness.

"It is I, Papa," Penelope said as she crossed the room, carrying a tray with a tempting array of fruit, the newspaper, and his morning pot of tea. Coffee had been forbidden, and she hoped he would not make another fuss. She had begun to wonder if it wouldn't simply be easier on him to allow him to have one cup in the morning. Certainly it would be easier on her. If she had her way, she'd ban the newspapers instead, since coffee could not possibly affect his temper any more than the threat of Louisiana sugar did. Placing the tray on the nightstand so that she could draw back the mosquito netting, she helped him prop himself up on his pillows before placing the tray across his lap.

It pained Abner to look at his aging daughter. She had buried the little girl he adored so long ago in mounds of fat. "What is this Yasushi tells me?" he asked, knowing he would get her goat. "We have two young ladies as guests and you did not inform me?" He forked a piece of pineapple and popped it into his mouth.

"Now, now, Pa," she replied soothingly, bracing herself for a tirade, ready to strangle Yasushi for his betrayal. She had sworn him to secrecy. Confined to his rooms, her father need never have known they were in the house. Had he heard their voices, she could always claim they were present on a short visit. "Do not get yourself all worked up," she said as if to a child. "That is the very reason I did not want you to know. First thing I know, you'd be trying to get out of bed too soon."

"Never too soon!" Abner exclaimed, annoyed by her tone. Brandishing his fork at her, he continued, "Sheer boredom will kill me quicker than dinner with two lovely ladies."

"Dr. Stevenson says you must have absolute bed rest, sir," she replied firmly. "We do not want you to have a recurrence, now do we?"

"Very well," he said, spearing a slice of banana. "Have them lunch with me here."

"Oh, I pray you, sir, do not insist!" she cried. "Think of the ants it would draw. The roaches! Why, your breakfast alone—"

"All right! All right!" he interrupted gruffly. "No refreshments, but do have them call—"

"Yes, yes," she replied. "After church, if they do not have other plans."

"Well, give me a chance to shave, girl!" He smiled, a not entirely pleasant expression.

Penelope shook her head as she watched him devour his breakfast. Propped against pillows, with his broad shoulders and deep chest, he did not look in the least frail.

"I hear the young one is the most attractive," he continued, his eyes lively. "A bit thin, but good hair and nice eyes."

"Yasushi said that?" she asked, wondering that a servant would speak of his betters in such a familiar fashion. But she knew her father. He could very well have asked a thousand questions, and with his preacher's way with people, he could get a brick wall to speak.

"The older one wears black all the time," he said, finishing his tea with an expression of distaste. "She lose a husband?"

"I really could not say, sir." Hoping to forestall this line of questions, she reached for the tray. "If I may be excused, sir, I have much to do this morning."

"You must not forget your promise, daughter," he said, taking the unopened newspapers from the tray.

She sighed heavily. "Yes, Papa."

"No, no!" Discarding the papers on the bed to grab her hand, he forced her to return the tray to his lap. " 'Yes, Papa' is not enough." Holding tight, he closed his eyes. "Say the words."

Penelope sighed again, but she knew better than to resist. "As God is my witness," she said, her tone sincere, "I will not allow anyone to bury Abner Tarkington until they are absolutely certain he is dead."

Preoccupied with her thoughts, Abigail did not notice that Jacqueline had used rats to increase the pouff in her chestnut hair, copying the latest mode, which caused her hat to perch at an angle that was a bit dashing for Honolulu. By the time she noticed what Jacqueline had wrought, it was too late to redo it without risking being late for church. With a pale pink sash encircling the tiny waist of her starched white, eyelet gown, a cameo broach at her throat and moonstones dancing in her ears, she might have stepped from a page in the latest issue of *The Ladies' Home Journal*. Having concentrated upon Abigail's new coiffure and dress, in the hopes of stilling her own troubled thoughts, Jacqueline was pleased with the results as she removed a new pair of gloves from their tissue and handed them to her mistress.

"Are these mine?" Abigail asked, clenching and unclenching her fist after drawing one on. "They seem too large."

"Oh, it is the fashion, miss," Jacqueline assured her. "Ladies wear the gloves large for the cooling."

Had Abigail been given the pair upon first arriving, she might have spurned them, thinking them unsightly. But she'd had time to observe that most women did wear their gloves wrinkled, and had experienced her own hands becoming uncomfortably hot in the skintight style that was de rigueur in New York. And with their high-necked, sleeves-to-the-wrist and floor-length gowns, loose-fitting gloves were the only concession to the heat available to a lady. "Where did you get them?"

"Miss Cunningham gives me money for her also—" Jacqueline paused. She wanted desperately to ask about Kinkade, but Abigail had been so absorbed, she had not dared interrupt. It was on the tip of her tongue to tell Abigail what she had seen, but a knock at the door precluded her effort. Maude entered without waiting for permission, ending her desire, since if she tattled at all, it would only be to Abigail.

Still annoyed by Abigail's bedtime remarks, Maude's expression was grim, but she wore a cool, white cotton gown instead of her usual widow's weeds. She refused to change her unfashionably severe hair, upon which her hat sat square.

Abigail felt overdressed by comparison.

Penelope wore her usual flower-printed frock, and although it was cinched at her ample waist, it more nearly resembled the tentlike garments, albeit tied in the middle, of the native wahines.

The Tarkingtons' best carriage was hitched to a matched pair and, with the driver ensconced upon his rightful seat, Penelope rode with her guests to the service at a more stately pace, as befitted the Sabbath. Matthew remained at home to share an hour of prayer with his father.

Had it been embowered by elm instead of palm, the gray stone church with its steeple piercing the sky might have been set in New England. Abigail had consented to attend services as much to hear the preacher as to conform to the rules of the household. Since it was unlikely that she would see Mr. Tarkington more than once, she wished to make the most of the unexpected interview scheduled after lunch, and she hoped for some comment from the minister that she might refer to in conversation.

But like preachers the world over, this one spent most of his sermon castigating those not in attendance for not being in attendance. They, of course, were not present to hear him. To complete the symmetry, he neglected to greet those who sat before him who had troubled to come and who might have appreciated his benediction. He also spent a lengthy portion of his sermon justifying the burning of Chinatown, accusing the filthy heathens of bringing it upon themselves by harboring the plague. The only time he waxed eloquent about God was when it came time to pass the collection plate, whereupon he made it clear how God was in great need of repairs to the steeple, which had lost some shingles in the last high wind. He might not survive the day without the congregants' generosity.

Her mission unaccomplished, and feeling not one whit closer to her Maker than she had when she entered despite the hymn sung fervently to the contrary, Abigail resolved to find a pretext for not attending services again in the unhappy event they were still in Honolulu the next Sunday.

▽

6

His LUNCH EATEN AND nap slept, Mr. Tarkington felt refreshed enough to receive his daughter's guests on the shaded lanai off his bedroom. His eyes had lit up at Abigail's entrance, and he had risen unsteadily from the *punee* to take her hand in greeting. Only somewhat less enthusiastically had he greeted Maude, and only after his guests were seated beside him in the high-backed wicker armchairs did he allow Penelope to fuss with the cushions to make him comfortable while reclining on the *punee*.

His color was poor underneath his tan, but Abigail was astonished that one supposedly near death could look so well.

Yasushi appeared, unbidden. Both father and daughter thinking the other had requested his presence, he was sent off to fetch pitchers of iced tea and lemonade. Penelope had questioned him closely, but he had vehemently denied tattling and, knowing her father, she had finally believed him.

"And to what do we owe the honor of your visit to our humble home, Miss Danforth?" Abner asked with a piercing glance at his daughter. He thought Abigail a perfect picture of a fortune hunter, and clever indeed to have so swiftly insinuated herself into the household. Even so, and although she was young enough to be his granddaughter, he would have liked nothing better than to be the first to bed her, there being no question in his mind that she was un-touched. The older one's purity was in considerable doubt.

"It was by my invitation, sir," Penelope responded swiftly. Her blush left her skin blotched rather than prettily coloring her cheeks.

"And what brings you girls to Hawaii?" he asked, ignoring Penelope's response.

"My companion and I had heard much of the fabled Sand-wich Islands, sir," Abigail replied truthfully enough, since she had been completely indifferent to their destination. "We availed ourselves of the opportunity to see them for ourselves."

Two women traveling alone could mean but one thing to Abner Tarkington. "Hunting for husbands, eh?" he said, never having been one for mincing words.

Maude did not have to see Abigail's expression to know that his remark had put her in a fume, and before she could find her voice and respond in some manner that she might later regret, Maude took the floor. Not wishing to offend a former minister, while allowing as how they were on a world tour, she alluded to her own recent widowhood without men-tioning she'd not been married. Nor did she mention that Abigail had caught her pseudo-husband's killer, or mention Abigail's ambitions to be a detective. She did respond truth-fully enough to his questions regarding Abigail's father and the status, and basis, of his considerable fortune. She also hinted that Abigail was recuperating from the trauma of a broken engagement, and while Europe was the favored des-tination for a girl of her station, since Abigail had spent so much time in London's finishing schools, she preferred ven-turing into the Pacific, with perhaps Australia an eventual destination.

The more Abigail watched Mr. Tarkington's responses while Maude was speaking, the more uneasy she became. While her father was gruff and distant, and she would have preferred a more friendly look in his eyes when he beheld her, Mr. Tarkington's eyes were intrusive. His grin, while friendly enough, more nearly resembled a leer. By the time Maude had completed her speech, all thoughts of asking him about God had flown, and she was ready for the interview to be at an end. But Yasushi returned with the refreshments. Although he tried to be unobtrusive, she insisted upon accepting the glass of tea in her hands, and thanked him with a smile instead of ignoring him as punctilio would have it, so that she could have a respite, however brief, from the conversation. She did not, however, follow Yasushi's exit to see him station himself within earshot in Mr. Tarkington's bedchamber.

"Have you introduced this lovely lady to Matthew?" Abner asked with a sidelong glance at Abigail.

"I met your son at the Daltons'," Abigail replied coolly, placing her glass upon the table that separated her from Maude.

"He would be a capital catch, you know."

"Since Miss Cunningham and I are soon leaving, sir, someone far luckier than I shall win the prize," she replied sweetly.

Knowing Abigail's use of sweet compliance to mask a will of iron, Maude pursed her lips to keep from laughing outright.

"Leaving!" Penelope exclaimed. "What of Kinkade?" she asked, before she could catch herself.

"He will be released Monday morning," Abigail said with assurance.

"Released?" Abner sat up on an elbow. "Where is he?" he asked. "For that matter, *who* is he?"

"Really, Papa, it is none of your concern." Penelope stood, motioning for Abigail and Maude to join her. "We have overstayed your strength already."

Maude stood, as did Abigail, only too pleased to comply.

"Who is Kinkade?" Abner insisted, shakily gaining his feet to observe the amenities.

"My father insists that Kinkade travel with me to ensure

my safety." Not wishing to have him use their leavetaking as an excuse to kiss her hand, Abigail took a step back. "He found Princess Lilliana's body yesterday, and the police have seen fit to hold him."

Abner's face lost what little color it had and, reaching back with his hands to be sure the couch was near, he sat down heavily.

"Papa!" Rushing to her father's side, Penelope pulled a vial of smelling salts from her pocket and held it under his nose. "See what you have done?" she cried, glaring at Abigail and Maude. "I pray you leave at once before you kill him."

Abigail and Maude glanced at one another. Maude's silently raised eyebrow clearly indicated her feelings that there was nothing to gain by remaining. Abigail's imperceptible shrug conveyed her agreement and, with sympathetic murmurs attesting to their concern, they obeyed Penelope's command with all due speed.

As the Tarkingtons' rooster crowed Monday into existence, Abigail stretched and yawned, and covered her ears with a pillow. But her thoughts followed her into the relative silence and, more irritating than the cock's crow, the unanswered questions kept her awake. There was nothing for it but to rise, dress, and visit Kinkade in jail.

She had finished her ablutions with the water pitcher, and selected her khaki riding costume with split skirts and a small straw hat with streamers, by the time Jacqueline appeared with a parcel meant for Kinkade instead of her morning tea.

Cheeks aflame with embarrassment, Jacqueline handed over the neatly tied package, the handiwork of Yasushi, whose tiny room Kinkade had shared so briefly. Most house servants went home at night, thus few houses had servants' quarters. Although the Tarkingtons' was an exception, Kinkade had merely been provided with a cot, a pallet actually, for it had lain on the floor, unsupported by legs or springs, with mosquito netting temporarily tacked upon the wall. His belongings had remained in their suitcases, now stacked along a wall, since no drawers or closet space had been provided, and the mattress and net had been stored away.

With Yasushi at her elbow, Jacqueline had stood in the doorway, staring at the stacked valises, wondering where to begin the search for those items he might need. The Japanese seemed to sense her difficulty and, without words, it was he who had examined those bags, which contained such underneath garments that men wore, and extracted same, shielding them from her view while wrapping them. But it was Jacqueline who had opened the square, hard-sided valise that seemed most likely to contain his hairbrushes and shaving gear. As indeed it had. But it had also contained bottles of Hair Tonic Restorer to encourage growth, Old Reliable Hair and Whisker Dye to hide the gray, and Hair Elixir to make the result more lustrous. Until that moment, she had believed women to be the vain sex, and she was by turns embarrassed and awash with guilt at having invaded his privacy, all the while wondering if his preoccupation with his hair was new and angered by the suspicion that it was. And amused.

She was not so amused when Abigail declared that her embarrassing experience had been for naught since she intended to secure his release and therefore he would have no need for supplies.

By the time Miss Cunningham joined them Jacqueline had buttoned Abigail into her riding costume and had put her hat in place. She was much relieved when neither lady bothered to question her about the parcel's contents. And dismayed by Maude's suggestion.

"You should take Jacqueline with you," Maude said, pointing a finger at the tiny maid.

The last thing in the world Jacqueline wanted to do was face Kinkade, but of course she could not voice a protest without revealing her reason. Crossing her fingers behind her back, she prayed for Abigail's refusal, which, since she was dressed for riding, was not unlikely.

"Taking the phaeton would only slow me down," Abigail responded as she stood.

"Then allow me to go with you," Maude insisted. "You will be entering upon a male preserve, and it is unseemly that you arrive unaccompanied."

"Oh, come, come, Miss Cunningham," Abigail said. "The men you speak of so suspiciously are empowered to uphold the law. They are unlikely to offend common decency."

"Ah, but if you place yourself at their mercy by failing to observe propriety, can they be blamed if they do?"

Abigail sighed impatiently. "Kinkade will be there."

"He is their prisoner!" Maude exclaimed. "That will only make your situation the more ambiguous." She shook her head disapprovingly. "And then you appear, riding astride—"

"Ah, that is what this quarrel is about!" Abigail interrupted heatedly. "Where are your eyes?" she cried. "Have you not noticed that the women of Hawaii ride astride?"

"But they are brown-skinned natives, Miss Danforth!" Maude responded triumphantly, certain she had won the day. "Not well-bred Americans!"

Fan and reticule dangling from her wrists, Abigail strode to the door. With one hand on the knob, she turned to face Maude. "If I allowed my breeding to dictate my actions, Miss Cunningham, I daresay I would not be going to Kinkade's rescue at all, now would I?" Before Maude could respond, she was out the door, slamming it resoundingly behind her.

Fortunately for Abigail, Officer Drew Miller of the large mustache was on hand to greet her arrival at the stationhouse. While more than one officer would have known Miss Tarkington on sight, not all who were now on duty had been present when the princess's body had been brought in, and except for those men, none would have known this strange girl who arrived alone, astride a horse, and entered the stationhouse with such unladylike self-assurance. There might have subsequently occurred some unpleasantries until the matter of her unassailable social connections had been established.

As it was, Officer Miller was able to intercept her at the sergeant's desk and pull two chairs in front of his desk in the corner, where she was made comfortable until Kinkade could be called in.

She had not long to wait before, accompanied by only one officer, the handcuffed Kinkade appeared.

"Thank you for coming, Miss Danforth," he said listlessly, slumping into the chair next to her.

"Can you not remove those cuffs, Officer Miller?" she asked with her most winsome smile, satisfied that Kinkade had been sufficiently chastised. "Surely you cannot believe that he means to escape?"

Miller shook his head. "Sorry, Miss Danforth, not as long as he sticks by his confession."

Abigail glared at Kinkade, but staring at his cuffed hands, he seemed not to notice. Instead of querying him, she turned her attention to Miller. "Do you know how she died?" she asked.

Again, Miller shook his head. This time he also stroked his mustache nervously before responding. "We had to release the body for burial."

"What?" Abigail exclaimed. "Was there no postmortem done?"

"I do not quite know how to say this without offending your delicate sensibilities, Miss Danforth, but ah—" Miller hesitated, unable to go on.

Understanding his dilemma at once, Abigail replied, "I suppose in this heat, that is, unless you packed the body in ice—"

"Well, that is not the whole of it, ma'am," Officer Miller said, much impressed with Abigail's aplomb. By now, most of the girls of his acquaintance would have swooned. Since she seemed so calm, he continued, "It was going to be impossible to prove any foul play since she was pretty well chewed by the fish."

With a guttural moan from deep inside, Kinkade doubled over, and before anyone knew what was happening, was violently sick on the floor.

Abigail shrieked. Sweeping her skirts aside before they were contaminated, she stood and stepped to the far side of her chair until his spasms passed. The officer who had escorted Kinkade in ran for some rags, while Officer Miller turned his back and, cursed with a weak stomach of his own, tried to control his own desire to retch.

Pulling a perfumed handkerchief from her reticule, Abigail held it to her nostrils against the stench while Kinkade was led away to be cleaned off and the officers mopped up the mess.

She had no sooner settled herself in the chair than Kinkade was returned. "Are you all right?" she asked, truly concerned. For the first time she began to appreciate how stricken he must have been by Princess Lilliana's death, and resolved anew to avoid falling in love at all costs.

Kinkade shook his head sorrowfully. "Oh, Miss Danforth," he said, his voice husky. "Find out who did that to her, I pray you."

"Who might have known you were going to meet her there?" Abigail asked, realizing that she could not disappoint him no matter how much she desired to quit the islands.

"That large Hawaiian who tried to attack me might have known. He was there when we met. And he saw us together in town."

"In town?" Abigail exclaimed, horrified. "How many times had you seen this—this princess?"

"Twice."

"Twice?" Abigail was more horrified still. How a man could be so wretched over the death of someone he had met but twice was beyond her comprehension. "And you would remain in jail for her?" she asked, incredulous.

"Until the end of time, Miss Danforth," he replied gravely. "If it takes you that long to find her killer."

A derailed streetcar, with its attendant snarl of vehicles as everyone disembarked, the male passengers to shout instructions at one another over the driver's swearing at the hapless donkeys while heaving the trolley back on the tracks, delayed Abigail's return to the Tarkingtons'. The resultant traffic jam had served to spook her high-strung thorough-bred, and her concentration thus focused upon riding her mount through the added tangle wrought by a pleasure vehicle driven by inexperienced hands that had upset a lumber wagon's cargo, while quacking, wing-flapping ducks that had escaped from their basket were chased by their owner cursing in Chinese, and amused pedestrians jeered loudly, adding unwanted advice, she'd had little time for contemplation.

It was with no little relief that she handed a wild-eyed Crosspatches over to the Tarkingtons' stableboy and, reluctant to face Maude or Penelope and their attendant questions until she had quieted her nerves, she decided to forgo lunch in exchange for a stroll through the garden. If memory served, there was a bench in a cove of trees that would prove a perfect spot of solitude to collect her agitated thoughts.

Leaving word at the kitchen not to expect her, she swiftly made her way across the expanse of lawn. The sun had chased away the mosquitoes, and a breeze had risen to mitigate its heat, creating an entirely pleasant day, which, after her nerve-wracking ride, even Abigail appreciated. Reaching the welcome shade of the trees, she slowed her step as she turned down the path toward the remembered bench. She had not gotten far when she became aware of a sound that was neither breeze nor bird. She stopped to listen. Her breath still, she heard a low moan that might have issued from something mortally injured. Unable to discern whether the sound came from an animal or human and unfamiliar with the island's wildlife, she hesitated. What if she stumbled upon an injured creature that would be rightfully unappreciative at the interruption, and attack? She shuddered, and seriously entertained the thought of returning to the house. Her caution lasted but a moment, overcome by her curiosity and a desire to help. Screwing up her courage, still holding her breath, she tiptoed toward the sound. As it grew louder, she suspected that it was coming from somewhere near the bench she sought. And indeed, as she peered around the banyan that hid the bench from view, she saw a man sitting upon it, elbows on knees, holding his head in his hands. It looked, and sounded, for all the world as if he was crying. She could scarcely believe her eyes.

Taking the necessary steps backward to conceal herself from his view should he look up, Abigail stood transfixed. Men did not cry. They professed to love. Certainly they got angry. And they could hate, and be warlike. And presumably hurt. But cry? Never. Never had she seen her father come close to shedding tears. Or either of her twin brothers. Or any other male of her acquaintance. Perhaps upon the loss of a great love, a man might shed a tear, but even then would he not seek the privacy of his rooms so that no one could witness his weakness? Then Abigail realized that she had sought this very spot for its solitude. As had he. As the intruder, it was clearly incumbent upon her to leave. But as she turned to go she could not help but wonder who it was that was in such deep distress. What catastrophe would be so overwhelming that it had precipitated the loss of his manhood?

Her glance had been so fleeting, and his features hidden, she had been certain only of his gender. Certainly she would not embarrass him by coming upon him now, but perhaps at some later date she might offer her assistance. But only if she could know his identity.

Retracing her few steps on tiptoe, she peeked around the tree. Again, she could tell little from his bent-over position except that he was male. And blond. Then he removed one hand from his face to reach for a handkerchief. It was Matthew.

Stunned, she ducked behind the tree. As she slowly turned to leave him to his private shame, she heard him blowing his nose, a clear indication that his crisis was near its end, or so it would have been in the case of a feminine bout of weeping. The desire to know what had pushed him to such an unprecedented act stopped her in her tracks. After all, she was no longer in danger of witnessing his tears. But it would be unseemly to see him wiping his eyes, so how to approach so that he could hear her coming and be done with his handkerchief?

She hit upon the idea to sing, but immediately discarded it. While she had a rich and melodious speaking voice, she could not carry a tune. Ah, but she could hum, she thought. But what? It seemed inappropriately gay, given his obvious grief, to use a modern tune. Swiftly settling upon a hymn from Sunday's service, she cleared her throat and, just before nonchalantly strolling from behind the tree, began to hum her best approximation of "Nearer My God to Thee."

▽

7

"MISS DANFORTH!" MATTHEW EXCLAIMED, pocketing his handkerchief as he stood to greet her. "And where is Miss Cunningham?" he asked with a shaky smile. He found her athletic riding costume most unattractive, and since he could not bestow an honest compliment he felt awkward, in addition to wondering if she had seen him cry.

Impelled by her curiosity, Abigail had utterly forgotten the compromising position she would be in were she caught with him alone in such an obvious trysting place. "Why, Mr. Tarkington!" she exclaimed with no pretense at being flustered as, in truth, she suddenly was. "I am quite alone." Chafing anew at the necessity of being accompanied by a chaperon, she sighed heavily and, not bothering to unfurl her fan, reluctantly turned to leave as propriety dictated she must.

"Oh, Miss Danforth, do not go, I beg you." Taking a quick step toward her, he reached out and touched her lightly upon the arm.

Shocked by his forward behavior, which she feared she might have encouraged by appearing before him by herself, she whirled to face him, ready to speak her mind about men who took advantage of the gentle sex.

As quickly as he had touched her, he withdrew his hand,

placing both behind his back like a naughty schoolboy. His handsome face crumpled with concern. "I realize our situation here is a delicate one," he said earnestly, "but since the Lord has answered my prayers—"

"I beg your pardon?" Abigail drew herself to her full height.

Withdrawing his hands from behind his back, he held his arms wide as if to embrace her. "You are the answer to my prayers!"

"Mr. Tarkington!" Knowing his recent past to have been worrisome, and having just witnessed his complete breakdown, faced with his zealous reference to the deity, she wondered if he might not be a trifle mad. Grasping her skirts slightly from behind in one hand, she prepared to flee.

"I asked God for a sign," he cried before she could turn away. His hands still outstretched, his gaze heavenward, he continued fervently, "And here you are!"

Poised for flight, Abigail glanced back at him. He seemed harmless enough, if a bit crazed, and her curiosity got the better of her. "I do not understand, sir," she said, genuinely puzzled.

Lowering his hands to his sides, he gazed at her with a longing that more properly belonged to a bereft lover. "You were at the ready to help me once."

His rudeness in rejecting her offer still rankled, especially since she had wasted so much time learning about poisonous insects, fish, and plants, all useless knowledge now unless she had another case requiring it before her memory failed. Abandoning civility, she made no attempt to keep annoyance from her tone as she replied. "You made it perfectly clear that you had no desire for my help!"

Hands once again behind his back, he replied, "I understand from Father that you are planning to leave Hawaii soon?"

Since he seemed to have calmed himself, she released her skirts. Not wishing to reveal that her plans were in disarray, she signified that his information was correct with a silent nod.

Wanting nothing more than to fling himself at her feet, Matthew forced himself to move a few steps away. As much as her answer meant to him, he could not look at her directly, but focused instead upon the tangled thicket that concealed them from view. "I wonder if I might prevail upon you to reconsider your plans for departure."

"To what purpose?" Abigail asked, with some asperity. She had tarried long enough, and was becoming restless with the necessity of breaking up their compromising situation.

"I fear you will think me a coward," he said, gazing at his feet.

Since his assessment was brutally accurate, given his bout of tears, she did not know how to respond. "There is no one alive who does not fear something," she said, embarrassed by her own triteness.

"How understanding you are." He glanced at her gratefully.

Only too aware how undeserving she was of the compliment, Abigail blushed.

Matthew paused, his manner grew solemn, his voice hushed. "I fear it is true that I am being poisoned, Miss Danforth." What little color was left in Matthew's face drained away, and for one awful moment, Abigail feared he might also swoon like a girl, but instead he turned away and strode to the edge of the clearing.

"I must be on my way, Mr. Tarkington," she said, turning toward the banyan tree, and the path to the house.

"Yes, of course, you must," he said. But before she could reach the tree, he dashed forward to stand in front of her, blocking her path. "Oh, Miss Danforth, I do not want to die!" he cried. "I pray you find out who is poisoning me!"

Abigail looked directly at him, her gaze fierce. "Do not dally with me, sir," she said, her voice flat. She had not cared for Matthew's father and his predatory glances and suspicions regarding husband hunting. If the fruit did not fall far from the tree, working closely with his son might prove complicated, not to say stormy, at least until she set them both straight. Yet, to be fair, it was much too soon to condemn the son for the father's sins. And his predicament was a cruel one.

He returned her gaze unflinchingly. "Never have I been more earnest," he replied, his hand to his heart.

Her gaze never left his face. "Once embarked upon a case it is not my practice to stop until I have an answer, no matter the consequences."

"I understand," he said, his gaze locked with hers.

"I have many questions to put to you—"

"Ask away!"

"I cannot, at this moment!" she replied briskly. "I have tarried too long as it is!"

"Name a time, Miss Danforth," he replied eagerly. "I shall be there."

Abigail searched his face. The fear she detected in his eyes disturbed her. Could he go the distance without changing his mind again? Yet his fate was bleak if she did not intervene. "Very well," she replied. "Shall we meet after dinner?" Not deigning to wait for an answer, she continued. "After our interview, with Miss Cunningham in attendance, of course, you shall have my answer." Abigail turned to leave.

Again, Matthew had the temerity to touch her arm. "I pray you, do not leave."

Abigail whirled about and glared at him.

"Do not mistake my meaning, Miss Danforth," he said, quickly withdrawing his hand. "I only meant that I shall be going back to the house now. It is obvious to me that you must have been seeking some measure of solitude or you would not have found your way to this spot. That I happened to be here, while fortunate for me, has usurped your chance for some privacy. I am much in your debt." His smile was most gracious as he nodded his head. "Allow me to be the one to leave." And with that, he was gone.

Abigail stood for a moment, listening until she was certain he would not return, then settled herself gratefully upon the bench, automatically arranging the folds of her skirts at their most becoming angle even though it was unlikely that anyone would see them. Impressed with his generosity, her thoughts in turmoil, she ignored the beauty that surrounded her. The cheerful chirping of birds annoyed rather than delighted her, as they disturbed her concentration. Rather than the serenity that she had so desperately needed to figure out the next steps necessary to free Kinkade, she had instead been met with yet another mystery to solve. And now, rather than leaving this overgrown jungle of an island with its lascivious profusion of romantic settings, much to her dismay, she was stuck. At least until she freed Kinkade. Did she really care to stay any longer to help Matthew? And yet, if she did not, what of the progress of her career? Could she rightfully consider herself a professional if she allowed her personal dislike of a place so disturb her that she would refuse to take on a client? But before she could consider her status as detective with a genuine client, she had to concentrate upon bailing out her servant who had placed her in a most ridiculous position.

After a few minutes' quiet reflection, the obvious became so obvious that she was annoyed anew with herself for thinking that she had needed privacy to figure it out. Of course, she needed to find out more about Princess Lilliana. Was she connected with the royal family? Penelope had implied that she was not. Who might profit from her death? And who was that large Hawaiian man who had barged in, threatening to attack Kinkade? A phone call to Officer Miller should solve the question of his name and whereabouts, as well as provide answers to her questions regarding the princess.

She bit her lower lip, and her eyes grew dark as she realized that she had allowed Kinkade's emotional reaction to affect her to such an extent that she had neglected to garner elementary information before quitting the stationhouse. It disturbed her deeply that she had unwittingly allowed herself to become so upset at Kinkade that she had wished to escape the scene before doing what was clearly her duty. Of course, she could telephone Officer Miller. And would. But she dreaded to think how inefficient he was going to believe her to be, if not downright incompetent, for not having asked him those questions when they were face-to-face. She despaired of subduing her own emotions so that they no longer interfered with her intellect.

And add to that, Matthew. What had changed his mind? Or more important, had someone else made up his mind for him in the first place, then changed it for him? If he were so in thrall to another, could he be trusted to act, or think, for himself?

And how to tell Maude?

Recalling how she had left the house with such certitude that she would return with Kinkade, she blushed to think of Maude's triumphant reaction when she appeared emptyhanded. Moreover, while she still hoped she might have Kinkade released soon, which would enable them to leave, she had no idea how long it would take to discover who was trying to kill Matthew. If she took his case. But most vexing of all, how was she going to tell Maude about speaking to Matthew without revealing that she had seen him alone? Maude might never let her hear the end of it, let alone get past the indiscretion long enough to address the problems at hand.

And Maude very nearly did just that. Recounting every time Abigail had ever put herself in jeopardy of rendering herself unmarriageable by sullying her reputation, Maude vented her opinion while pacing from her bedroom to the lanai attached thereto, and back. Knowing that to interrupt or protest would merely result in lengthening her companion's interminable tirade, Abigail stood at the railing on the lanai and remained silent. And contrite.

At length, having said her piece, Maude stood before Abigail, a questioning frown on her face.

Having long ago stopped listening, Abigail had all she could do to refrain from yawning, which would have been a disaster, precipitating another lecture regarding the seriousness of her breach in conduct. "I do understand, Miss Cunningham," she hastened to say, waving her hand at the cushioned rattan chairs, indicating that they both might be more comfortable seated. Hoping to change the topic from her own mistakes, as they settled themselves in the chairs, she continued, "The police did not even do a postmortem."

Maude paused. Loath to move to a new subject until she was certain she had impressed Abigail with the gravity of her transgression, she realized that they had much to discuss with very little time alone to do so. She therefore refrained from pressing her point, and instead replied, "Do they know how she died?"

"Presumably by drowning. Her body was—ah—" Recalling Kinkade's reaction, Abigail glanced appraisingly at Maude before continuing, "Shall we say the worse for wear, having shared the pond with some hungry fish."

"I see," Maude said placidly enough, as if the information were a simple delivery of facts holding no horror.

Abigail paused thoughtfully. "Do you realize he only saw her twice?" She could not keep the wonderment from her voice.

"What is so unusual about that, pray?" Maude looked at her sharply. "Where are your powers of observation, Miss Danforth? He worked for your father for twenty years. When has he ever had a moment to fall in love? It seems obvious to me that he could be smitten beyond recovery quite easily upon one sight, given that the girl was an exotic beauty as I hear tell the princess was."

"But you thought Jacqueline . . ." Abigail let her voice trail off as she waved a hand suggestively, indicating a connection between the two.

"Ah, yes, Jacqueline." Maude sighed. "I wonder how she is taking this."

"That is the least of my worries!" Abigail replied with a dismissive wave of the same hand.

Fingertips to lips, Maude cleared her throat unnecessarily in hopes of cleansing the triumph from her voice. "Perhaps she could be prevailed upon to take that parcel to him?"

Suspecting that Maude was crowing over being right, Abigail glared at her without responding.

"I thought you might enjoy the sea air and have made inquiries about passage on a three-masted schooner," Maude said much too sweetly. "Have you any idea how long all of this will take?"

"I have no idea, Miss Cunningham." Abigail shrugged, ignoring the jibe. "If I take Mr. Tarkington's case, it could be weeks," she continued, emphasizing the word "if."

Maude shook her head. "Having met the senior Mr. Tarkington, I am most heartily sorry I suggested that you have anything to do with the family."

"You, too, eh?"

Maude nodded her agreement. "What changed Mr. Tarkington's mind?"

"Believe what you like," Abigail said, suddenly cross. "I was well aware of my compromised situation, and I did not take the time to ask him," she added heatedly. "We have an appointment to see him after dinner."

"We?" Maude asked with arched brow.

"I must not be alone with him, remember?" Abigail responded ironically, having just suffered a lecture upon the issue.

Maude shrugged. "Will his sister join us?"

"I should think not," Abigail said, rising. "The two of us will be a formidable combination, I should think." Her grin was wicked. "For such a misogynist, two of us should be all he could bear at one time."

Abigail's description of the derailment had the unwitting effect of dissuading Jacqueline from riding the trolley. No amount of cajoling could persuade her to board so untrustworthy a vehicle. Abigail had been forced to draw detailed directions and, the map tucked into the cuff of her glove, Kinkade's parcel in the basket between the handlebars, Jacqueline set out for the stationhouse on her bicycle. While the journey was the longest she had undertaken on her two-wheeler, just one wrong turn, which ended up being all right since it was in the same direction, only a different block instead of the one recommended, and she was there.

Invigorated by the exercise, her color was high, and, even had she not been expected, more than one officer would have had an appreciative glance for the diminutive maid. But Abigail had called and, after speaking at length with Officer Miller, had warned him of Jacqueline's arrival, and more than one man had anticipated it with much curiosity. A confessed murderer of a beautiful princess, visited by no less a personage than Miss Tarkington, working for a remarkably beautiful, if a mite too intelligent, girl, and now a maid visits him, and she turns out to be quite pretty as well, Kinkade was a curio among the policemen. There was much speculation among them as to how a middle-aged man with such a fierce physiognomy could be surrounded by so many lovely or, failing good looks, well-connected girls.

On tiptoe, Jacqueline handed the desk officer the parcel for Monsieur Kinkade. Seeing the parcel safely passed to another for a thorough inspection, mission complete, she turned to leave. But before she could take a step, she was invited to the absent Officer Miller's desk. Given the special nature of his incarceration, although handcuffed, Kinkade had been brought out of his cell, and was waiting for her, Officer Miller having assumed that Abigail had wished it, and had just forgotten to ask, as she had so prettily admitted to having forgotten her questions.

Believing herself to be acting as courier, Jacqueline had not expected to see Kinkade at all. His haggard appearance added to her confusion, and she was unable to command enough English to greet him.

Kinkade stood at her approach. Trying to mask his embarrassment at having her see him in handcuffs, his voice was brusque. "What are you doing here?"

"I brought you some—" She gestured toward the sergeant's desk where she had relinquished his package, and completed her sentence by touching her face where whiskers might be.

Nodding at her that she should sit, Kinkade took his chair.

The officer assigned to guard him shrugged and, believing Kinkade to be innocent of any crime, moved away to give them some modicum of privacy in the crowded room.

"I suppose I should thank you—" Kinkade began, intending to apologize for his gruff demeanor.

"Miss Danforth made me do it," Jacqueline interrupted, angered that he would equivocate about owing her the courtesy of thanking her for the trip. And not so much as a question about how she had managed it.

"Well, thank her, then," he replied, apology forgotten.

"She has much anger with you, you know."

"Well, I am angry, too!"

"At Miss Danforth?" Jacqueline was shocked.

"No, imbecile!" Kinkade glared at her as if she were daft. "At the killer who drowned the princess!"

"I knew you did not do it!" she exclaimed, relieved that he was not angry with their mistress.

Even though the police officer had stationed himself at some distance, he could not help but overhear Jacqueline's comment and, pretending to be tired, pulled up a chair and, back turned toward them, sat close by. While he might believe Kinkade innocent, it would nonetheless behoove him to listen in should the man say something to substantiate his confession.

Noticing the officer's movements, Kinkade lowered his voice. "How can you be so sure I am innocent?"

Afraid to say anything for fear she'd reveal she had followed him, Jacqueline hung her head without replying.

"See!" Kinkade sat back righteously.

"Oh, but you could not do the murder, monsieur!" she cried. "You are much too kind."

"What if she had taken a liking to me?" Kinkade leaned forward. "She had agreed to meet me, don't you see?"

"No, I do not see!" Jacqueline exclaimed, genuinely puzzled.

"What if I made someone jealous enough so that he killed her!"

Knowing the secret vanity of his hair, and astounded by his arrogance that led him to believe that a beautiful young girl could find him attractive, Jacqueline quite forgot how attractive she herself considered him to be. Unable to sort her feelings, she could not respond.

Kinkade did not notice her confusion as he continued gravely, "I know how I'd feel if someone touched her."

Still unable to decide whether to laugh, cry, or scream, Jacqueline searched for a handkerchief in her reticule.

"If my attentions inspired the killer, then I am equally guilty."

"Oh, monsieur, how can you think that?" she said, finding her voice at last, pressing a handkerchief to her nose.

"Because it is true, Miss Bordeaux," Kinkade said, standing to leave. "Because it is true."

▽

8

THE RAINS CAME DURING DINNER. Yasushi dashed into the dining room to help Matthew shutter the *makai*, or sea side, from whence they came. The lights fed by electricity flickered as alarmingly as did the candles that prettied the table, but the squall swiftly passed, having the salubrious effect of blowing the mosquitoes away. Thus Abigail, Maude, and Matthew were able to repair to the *mauka*, or mountain side, lanai, which had remained dry, when Penelope excused herself after dessert to go read to her father.

Despite the storm, or perhaps because of the excitement it had afforded, the dinner had gone swimmingly. Yet as the meal had progressed, Abigail had become more and more discomfited. Anticipating what was to follow when their discussion must of necessity turn to the serious matter of Matthew's predicament, she was concerned that their levity at table might make the transition difficult, if not impossible.

But more than the frivolous conversation, which she reluctantly indulged in, her very appearance made her uneasy. She and Maude had quarreled for the better part of an hour over what she should wear. Maude had argued that since Matthew had just seen her in such an athletic costume as a riding habit, she needed to balance the masculine impression she might have made by appearing as feminine as possible.

Abigail felt she should continue to dress more like the modern girl, the better to impress him with her seriousness. Only when Jacqueline had joined the fray with the incontrovertible fact that a blouse simply would not do for dinner, had she surrendered and, despite her continued misgivings, allowed herself to be persuaded to wear the most feminine gown in her wardrobe. Fashioned from gossamer cotton tucked with tiny rows of gathered lace, it made her look like a popular debutante with nothing more weighty on her mind than filling her dance card, and not at all like a detective.

In the end Abigail had succumbed because, in her heart of hearts, she enjoyed looking pretty, and resented the necessity of looking severe so that she would be taken seriously. However, as course had followed course, she had become more ill at ease as Matthew had become more and more attentive, and the glances he bestowed upon her more flirtatious. Little did she know that he had been suffering the torments of the damned with his leg at the beginning of the meal. But as the evening had progressed, the pain had eased, and he had attributed his momentary cure to her distracting charm.

Escorting them to the lanai, Matthew fussed over the seating arrangements, ostensibly providing for their comfort. Abigail was by turns amused and concerned to note that while he saw to it that her companion was ensconced upon the more comfortable *punee*, when Maude reclined into the pillows he provided, she was relegated to the shadows, out of the line of conversation. She was even more clearly pegged the gooseberry when he pulled his chair at an angle to face her own, putting his profile to Maude. All of which he had skillfully managed in order to provide himself with the possibility of exchanging a quiet word or two with her without the danger of being overheard by their chaperon. Abigail could not help but wonder how often he had practiced such maneuvers to have accomplished them so smoothly.

With equal smoothness, Yasushi laid coffee upon the table between them and, disappearing into the nearby dining room, took care to remain within earshot.

Myriad assorted insects chirruped their appreciation for the fresh-washed night, and for a fleeting moment Abigail wished they were gathered on the lanai to savor the fine evening. However, she could not risk Matthew's taking charge of the conversation the way he had the seating arrangements and lead them off into more pointless merriment; therefore she scarcely allowed him to settle himself in his chair before beginning her inquiry. "I do have many questions for you, Mr. Tarkington," she said, careful to smile most winsomely.

"I am your willing slave," he responded eagerly, as he was beginning to feel himself to be, having been utterly charmed by her lighthearted gaiety.

Abigail steeled herself. She realized that while he might be by nature, and training, a gallant gentleman, his use of his charm upon her was due to her girlish behavior during dinner. She feared his response would be quite different once her questions began in earnest. Knowing she'd not get far by asking him about his symptoms, and having learned her lesson at the stationhouse in the matter of beginning with the obvious, she decided she might as well use what she had been taught and plunge right in. Drawing a deep breath, she said, "Do you have any enemies, sir?"

"I?" Taken aback by the directness of her query, Matthew placed a hand to his breast. "Enemies?" he cried.

Although she appreciated the necessity of her role as chaperon, Maude had been nonetheless offended at being so summarily dismissed, and it was with some glee that she smothered a giggle at his having his vanity piqued.

Abigail gazed at him coolly.

"What must you think of me?" he asked, suddenly alarmed. Having discovered Abigail to be a normal girl, and consequently most attractive, he certainly did not want her to think ill of him.

"I think nothing untoward, sir, but is it not obvious to you that someone must mean you harm—"

Caught up as he was in his feelings for her, Abigail's logic was lost on him. "I am most heartily sorry that you think I am the sort of gentleman who would go around accumulating enemies," he replied, eager to correct such a negative impression.

"I would think that everyone has enemies," she said with a slight shrug to indicate that she thought it to be a common occurrence.

Matthew was aghast at her statement. That girls even thought of such things was foreign to him. Yet, upon reflection, he supposed that one girl might incur the anger of another in the case of a stolen suitor. Assuming Abigail might have been speaking from just such an experience, his tone held more than a casual interest as he asked, "Even you?"

"This is not about me," Abigail said with some asperity. Having incurred the wrath of some very important people who had put her life in danger because of it, she was beginning to wonder at Matthew's singular naïveté.

"Well, of course it is not about you," he said with a smirk. Since she was pretty enough to turn the head of any beau, he could well imagine every debutante in Honolulu being envious. She could make enemies of every one of them just by her arrival upon the scene. "What can you know about having enemies?" he asked, his voice filled with irony.

"It is my business to know, sir." She smiled sweetly, infuriated by his patronizing demeanor. "Solving murders is my chosen profession."

Matthew's jaw dropped. Caught up in how pretty Abigail was—how normal—he had quite forgotten that she aspired to being a detective.

"And she is very good at it, too," Maude chimed in from the shadows, her patience worn thin by his refusing to honor Abigail's questions with a direct answer.

"How morbid!"

Maude sat forward on one elbow to make sure she was heard. "You do not realize how very lucky you are, sir!"

"I daresay I am," Matthew responded, his tone ironic and not in the least chastened. "However, may I remind you girls that I am not yet dead?"

The irreverent thought that were he dead he'd be a good deal less difficult popped into Abigail's mind, and it was all she could do to refrain from saying it. But she suspected that his sense of humor did not extend to himself, and it might cost her the interview, if not his willingness to have her intervene. Certainly it would knock her interrogation, such as it was, off course. And while flattered by Maude's compliments, she would have preferred that Maude kept her remarks to herself, but telling her so in front of Matthew would merely sound churlish. Occupied with her thoughts, and aware that time was swiftly passing, she did not realize how she sounded when she said, "Well, then," her smile was sweet, making her remark seem all the more sarcastic, "have you any friends?"

Matthew could scarcely believe his ears. "I beg your pardon?" he cried in an injured tone.

"I cannot believe that you did not hear me, sir!" she exclaimed testily, intent upon keeping their interview on track.

"I cannot believe what I heard!" He twisted around to address Maude. "Did she actually question whether I have any friends?"

Maude cringed inside. Although she considered him arrogant, she could well understand why the young man might be offended, and gave him credit for not leaping up and leaving the scene at once. That he did not spoke a great deal for his self-control, especially since it was so obvious that he was attracted to Abigail. It must have distressed him mightily to have her suspect that he might be friendless. "I am certain Miss Danforth meant no offense, sir," she said reassuringly.

Abigail groaned. Matthew was proving to be even more difficult than she had expected. And now Maude took his part. "I merely wondered if perhaps you had a friend whom you might have harmed in some way," she said defensively.

"Harmed?" Matthew was indignantly. He drew himself tall in his chair as he spoke. "I would not be much of a gentleman if I went around harming my friends, now would I?"

"Perhaps harm is too harsh a term," Abigail replied with an impatient sigh. "Is there someone whom you have bested somehow?" She hastened to add, "Without meaning to, of course."

Matthew looked at her, his expression blank.

Maude groaned at her young friend's tactlessness, wondering that Abigail could not see how she was wounding Matthew by impugning his character.

"Did you get the better of someone somehow in a business deal?" Abigail suggested. "Beat him in a horse race—or surfing perhaps?"

Rendered speechless by the impertinence of Abigail's questions, Matthew turned again to Maude as if she might come to his defense.

Wondering why Abigail could not see the distress she was causing, Maude said, "I am certain that Mr. Tarkington is innocent of deliberately harming a friend, Miss Danforth."

Furious that Maude was taking Matthew's part, and annoyed by his refusal to cooperate, Abigail became even more determined to have answers, and her voice had an edge when she asked, "Might you have made someone jealous?"

"Miss Danforth!" Matthew laughed out of her amazement. Did she know something? Lighthearted banter about the green-eyed monster took up much time in ordinary conversations between gentlemen and ladies at parties, and was considered a social skill. But now she had hit close to the mark, and he wondered whether it was an accident, or if she knew something. "What can you mean?" he asked, hoping to find out what she knew.

Abigail blushed, and though the night was cool, she resorted to the use of her fan to conceal her emotions. Realizing

she was treading on delicate ground, she nonetheless persisted. "Perhaps you stole the heart of a maiden that a friend
of yours fancied?"

Worried now that she did know about him, he tried to
sound casual, as if he were genuinely teasing. "Who do you
have in mind?"

"Why, no one in particular, Mr. Tarkington," she replied,
trying to sound as though she were making light of the matter although she was in deadly earnest.

That he had just thought her capable of creating the same
emotion on a grand scale a moment ago did not occur to
him. Suddenly suspicious of her motives, he asked, "Why
would you want to know such a thing?"

"I need some information regarding your enemies, sir!"
Abigail exclaimed. "Since you insist that you have none, I
need to know who might have been your friend at one time,
yet been turned away for some reason. Jealousy is a powerful
motive for such a change!"

"What you ask is unseemly for me to answer!" he exclaimed with all the righteousness of one guilty as charged.

"Mr. Tarkington!" Abigail stood, all patience spent.

Matthew immediately got to his feet.

Abigail strode to the railing before turning to face him. "I
am only asking questions to try and find out who would have
a reason for poisoning you!"

Matthew was at her side in a trice. "Shhhhhhh!" Placing
fingertips to lips, he begged her to be quiet.

Abigail was unrepentant. She did, however, lower her
voice so that she could not be heard beyond the boundaries
of the lanai. "If you will not answer my questions, it is going
to be impossible for me to help you."

Maude caught her breath at the sight. The moonlight had
cast their figures into silhouette and the lovely girl and handsome young man looked like lovers discussing wedding plans
as they stood together at the railing. Realizing how distraught he must be at Abigail's questions, Maude forced
herself to rise from her comfortable position. Gaining her

feet, she crossed to them. "You must not view Miss Danforth as just an empty-headed girl, sir," she said earnestly as she drew near. "She is trying to help you."

Matthew was aghast. "Not think of her as a girl!" he exclaimed. "How is that possible?" Matthew gazed at each in disbelief.

"If you do not answer her questions, she will not be able—"

Abigail reached out her hand, touching Maude upon the arm to still her comment. "Perhaps Mr. Tarkington has leprosy, Miss Cunningham, and any effort on my part would be for naught."

With that, Matthew crumbled. Both Maude and Abigail stared as he gasped and, pulling a handkerchief from his pocket to hold to his face, stumbled to his chair. Flailing his free arm about, he indicated that they should sit so that he might be permitted to do so. Both hastened to oblige, Maude to regain her position on the *punee*, and Abigail to sit on the edge of the chair she had just quitted. Suspecting that she had given voice to his worst fear, Abigail was at a loss for words to alleviate his distress.

Handkerchief to his face, indulging in what seemed to be a sudden coughing fit, Matthew tried desperately to regain control. Fortunately for all, he was saved from the task of speaking by Yasushi's silent appearance asking if more coffee would be desired.

While immensely grateful for the timely interruption, Abigail did not fail to note that it was timely indeed. Not for the first time she wondered if the ubiquitous Japanese had not stationed himself nearby. And if so, why?

When the ladies declined his offer, Matthew pocketed his handkerchief while dismissing him with a wave of his other hand.

"I know this has been difficult for you, Mr. Tarkington," Abigail said before he could speak. Just in case Yasushi was lurking nearby, grateful for Matthew's foresight in arranging the chairs, she leaned forward so that only he could hear. "Would it be possible for you to get away for a while?"

Matthew looked at her as if she were daft. He shook his head. "Impossible," he said, his voice grim.

"But your life is at stake, sir!"

Matthew was adamant. "Much too much work at the mill."

"Then what if you stayed on the plantation? If your symptoms disappeared you would know beyond a doubt that you were being poisoned."

He shook his head. "My father is ill," he said. "I am taking his place in many matters, and I must report to him personally."

"Why can you not call him upon the telephone?"

"Many things we discuss are confidential in nature, Miss Danforth. The telephone operators would have the gossip spread all over Oahu in a matter of minutes."

"Then you would appear to be trapped, sir." Abigail leaned back in her chair thoughtfully. "Not ideal for your health, of course, but helpful if we are to catch the culprit."

"If only I had an enemy?" Matthew's tone was ironic.

"Perhaps you have no need for an outside enemy, sir," Abigail responded, her voice flat. "Poisoning is an intimate crime. Someone needs the opportunity as well as a reason to dispatch you. It is more likely to be administered by a family member or someone who has access to you." She paused but briefly before continuing, "And someone who would profit greatly by your death."

"Miss Danforth!" Matthew stood. "I say!"

Abigail gazed up at him calmly. "It would interest me to know what changed your mind about asking me to help you."

Matthew walked to the railing and stared out into the night for some time. Abigail was suddenly aware of how loudly the insects were singing. At length he turned to face her as he said with a dismissive shrug, "The pain."

Abigail gazed at him, trying to assess his sincerity.

He returned to stand by the table. "Will you help me?"

"I will let you know on the morrow," she replied. "First I must attend Princess Lilliana's funeral."

"Shall we go together?"

Abigail was surprised. "You are going?"

"All of Honolulu will be there, except her father," he replied. "It would not be politic to absent it."

Abigail was crestfallen. She had been counting upon the event of the funeral as an opportunity to meet Princess Lilliana's parents, and if all went well, to arrange for an interview. "Why might that be?" she asked.

"Oh, he is supposed to be a kahuna." Matthew shrugged.

"Might I ask what a kahuna is?"

"A holy man," he said. "Actually there are two kinds. The kahuna lapa'au are powerful healers. The kahuna 'ana'ana practices black magic." He shuddered. "Hawaiians believe that they can pray a person to death."

The sun was fast disappearing into the water when William, his huge, well-muscled body clad only in a loincloth, found the spot he had been searching for. Spectacular colors painted the clouds, but their beauty was lost on him as he closely examined the strength of the waves. No rocks for them to dash against here. A gentle slope of sand endured their onslaught, and returned them to the ocean when they were spent. Dropping his loincloth onto the beach, William walked out to meet one.

When the undertow threatened to pull him off balance, he raised his hands high and, taking a deep breath, closed his eyes and mouth, and dived headlong into an oncoming breaker. The water's force smashed the breath out of him. It burned his eyes, filling his mouth and nostrils. He was helpless but for an instant. His head emerged into a pocket of air and, gasping for breath, relishing his strength, he began to swim toward the horizon. But the first wave had dashed him off course and into the angle of another, larger one that submerged him entirely. Tossing him about on its insides at will, it washed him up into the shallow water, and would have deposited him on shore like so much seaweed had he not struggled to pull himself to his feet. Staggering back to where the undertow pulled at his legs, once again he dove in.

Thus he tried to outswim his grief.

The moon was high when he washed up on the beach for the last time, too exhausted to return. He lay on the sand moaning in pain, but not from the physical effort. His grief had won.

$\triangledown$

9

WEARY FROM THE PAST few days with the needlework required to alter one of Maude's black dresses to fit the smaller, thinner Abigail, Jacqueline could scarcely keep her eyes open as she stood behind her mistress, who was seated at her dressing table, and put the finishing touches to her coiffure. Having shorn the black straw hat, which was on loan from Maude, of adornment, Jacqueline had added black satiny streamers for the somber occasion. She pinned the hat flat atop Abigail's pompadour, and stepped back to observe the results.

Abigail was not pleased. "I look like I am at death's door," she complained, reaching up to shift the hat to a more becoming angle.

Far from offended, Jacqueline agreed with her mistress. Weeds did not become her, but there was nothing for it but to wear them for a funeral. That Maude, who stood in the doorway to the lanai, presumably to catch a breeze while waiting for Abigail to get ready, still preferred to gown herself in them was beyond her understanding. Stifling a yawn, she did not tarry when Abigail dismissed her.

The moment the door closed behind her maid, Abigail turned to face Maude, who remained in the doorway. "If it should happen that you are with me again when I am inter-rogating a client, I wonder if I might prevail upon you not to interfere?"

Maude shook her head. "Could you not see that every question you put to Mr. Tarkington offended him?"

"Alas." Abigail shrugged. "It was only after I asked him about enemies that I realized that he needed none." She pointed a finger at Maude. "Nonetheless, your taking his part did nothing to aid my inquiry, but rather made me look the fool."

"And did I not say inspiring things about you?" Maude said, moving into the room.

Retrieving her gloves from the top of the dressing table, Abigail concentrated upon drawing them on as she spoke. "All the more embarrassing, Miss Cunningham, since he was singularly unimpressed. You made it seem that I was pinning roses on myself."

"When the remarks came from me?"

"He might have thought I put you up to it."

Maude laughed. "I do not think his mind is as devious as yours. And to be frank with you," she added, "I believe that finding someone who might be poisoning him is an impos-sible challenge."

"Is that so?"

"I must admit I regret having gotten you into this mess."

"Well, we are stuck in this accursed place until I can remove Kinkade from jail." Parasol in hand, reticule and fan about her gloved wrists, Abigail moved toward the door. "And I fear Jacqueline would quit my employ if we moved back to the hotel."

"Can we not stay here?" Maude followed her.

Abigail paused at the door, hand on the knob. "We would no doubt be more welcome if Miss Tarkington felt I was doing something for her brother."

Maude was shocked. "You would deceive her for a place to stay?"

"Now it is my turn to be frank." Abigail took her hand

from the doorknob and lowered her voice. "If I am to be a consulting detective I need a crime to solve. As long as we cannot quit this dreadful place I might as well see if there is something I can discover that will ease Mr. Tarkington's situation."

"Have you a plan?" Maude asked, no longer surprised by Abigail's persistence.

Abigail lowered her voice further still. "Have you noticed Yasushi?"

Maude pulled back, her brows furrowed in puzzlement. "A model servant," she said. "The household is blessed to have him."

"Have you not noticed how he is always lurking about?" Abigail's voice was scarcely above a whisper.

"How else to serve?"

Abigail put her fingertips to her lips to indicate that Maude should speak more softly still. "How better to keep track of Mr. Tarkington?"

"But why?" Maude whispered. "You said yourself that the poisoner needs to profit. How could a servant profit?"

"Someone outside the household could be paying him." Hand on the knob once again, she said, "I shall need to put some questions to him as soon as we return."

Snapping in the brisk breeze, an American flag flew over Iolani Palace, branding Hawaii a territory. Haole businessmen viewed the sight with pride, and a delight not untinged by avarice. Most loyal Hawaiian subjects looked upon it with something less than enthusiasm, if not bitterness. No longer a home for the royal family, the palace was used primarily as an executive building for the provisional government, with the house of representatives meeting in the defunct throne room.

Indifferent to the political significance of the flag, neither was Abigail particularly impressed with the magnificence of the palace, having been privy to the noble houses in Europe. By those standards it was modest. As the grandest edifice in

Honolulu, it was opulent indeed, its many slender columns soaring two stories high, the whole crowned by a cupola fancy enough to please any potentate. The doors between what had been the blue room and the enormous dining room had been opened to accommodate those attendees at the funeral who had been invited to partake in refreshments.

By the time the Tarkington party drew up to the gates, the spacious drive leading to the palace steps was so clogged with vehicles that Abigail suggested they abandon the reception altogether since they'd no doubt be too late for the receiving line. She was much amazed when Penelope not only refused her suggestion, but did so with a heat she had never before displayed. Matthew saved the day by suggesting they quit the carriage and walk the remaining distance. Handing the ladies down, he was careful to see that Abigail and Maude walked in front of him while he followed close behind with Penelope on his arm.

The Tarkingtons stopped several times on the path to wave at acquaintances trapped in their carriages in the driveway. Matthew tipped his hat at the ladies, who returned his salute with somber nods and speculative glances at the two women who stopped alongside the brother and sister. One older couple, taking note of their superior progress, called to their driver to remain at a halt while they exited their carriage to join them. Abigail and Maude were introduced as houseguests.

Smiling gamely, Abigail endured their surreptitious glances. She knew that although they were too polite to say anything aloud, they could not help but be wondering how a foreign girl, whose servant had confessed to the murder of the very princess they were paying homage to, had managed to insinuate herself into the home of one of the most eligible men on Oahu. She suspected that few, if any, inhabitants of the island had read Dr. Arthur Conan Doyle's work and it was unlikely that they knew what the infant science of detection was, much less the definition of a consulting detective. Therefore, the moment the amenities were dispensed with she hurried ahead. As long as they were going to attend, she wanted to make the best use of her time by trying to locate William.

Maude took care to catch up and be in step with her as they started up the steps to the palace. Leaning close so as not to be overheard by the Tarkingtons, who trailed behind, she said, "Everyone seems to think that there must be something between you and Mr. Tarkington."

Abigail blushed furiously. Maude was right. Being seen together in this crowd, all of Honolulu would have them paired, a development she had not foreseen. Without answering Maude, lifting her skirts, she mounted the remaining steps with an unladylike speed, as if in doing so she might outrun the speculation.

Not only could she not outrun it, it grew worse with every introduction as the foursome made their way through the crowd in the enormous center hall with its paneling and sweeping grand staircase of koa wood the color of pulled taffy. Once into the blue room proper, ever on the alert for William, she paid scant attention to most of the new people she met until she was introduced to Bruce Dalton, and had her answer to Penelope's desire to attend the reception no matter how long it took to gain the palace, or how late they were. Bruce had been absent from the Daltons' dinner party. One of the sons of the host, business on Maui had kept him away. Not as tall as Matthew, only a hairsbreadth taller than Penelope for that matter, everything about him was thick. Not fat or heavy, Abigail thought, but his brows, beard, and nose as well as his fingers and waist were thick. Everything, that is, except his wit, which was as sharp and as penetrating as his glance, and as disconcerting as the senior Mr. Tarkington's.

Abigail was amazed to note that Penelope was positively simpering at the sight of him, since upon meeting her she had consigned the woman to the category of confirmed old maid past her prime, if the poor thing had ever had one, with no interest in men. Her extra width had the advantage of casting doubt upon her age, since a round chin tended to mask the telltale indications of the entrance into a third decade.

Mr. Dalton's beard served much the same purpose, and since no gray marred his hair, and it was as thick as any youngster's, it was difficult to say whether he was old enough to be a proper suitor, should he be so inclined.

Her skin blotched where a becoming blush should be, Penelope made it painfully clear that she wished he would be inclined, thereby creating the worst possible impression if she truly desired him. Abigail's heart went out to the unattractive woman. Motherless herself, at least her father had sent her to finishing schools. While she had been hopeless at playing the piano and singing, at least she had learned deportment and the use of the fan and, most important, how to deport herself to the best advantage in the company of men so that she was equipped to do battle in the arena of snaring a husband. From the way Penelope dressed, Abigail wondered if the woman even possessed a girlfriend who might advise her, and it entered her mind to volunteer Jacqueline's services.

Abigail was embarrassed for her anew as Bruce lingered over Maude's hand in greeting while Penelope's fond gaze never left him.

Then, rather than take Abigail's fingertips in greeting, Bruce took her whole hand in his, squeezing it suggestively while gazing deep into her eyes with a look that made her queasy, much like the senior Tarkington's. Instantly repulsed, she pulled her hand away as Penelope spoke. "Did you receive an invitation?" she asked anxiously.

His gaze lingered upon an embarrassed Abigail as he replied, "I have not had time to open the mail, Miss Tarkington."

"The Tibaults are giving a croquet party this Friday, weather permitting," Penelope said eagerly. "Will you be there?"

Not looking at Penelope, but directly at Matthew, he replied, "How long are these beautiful girls staying with you, you lucky dog?"

Matthew blushed. He disliked Bruce, but knew how his sister doted on him. "I really could not say, sir," he responded. He, too, was aware of how he and Abigail were being considered by all who met them today. Anything he said by way of hoping she and Maude would stay could easily be misconstrued, and land him in a breach of contract suit. He smiled uneasily.

Abigail recognized Matthew's dilemma at once. "Our plans are unformed at the moment, Mr. Dalton," she said swiftly.

Matthew glanced at her gratefully, even as he hoped she would stay.

With an overlong, speculative glance at Abigail, Bruce turned to Penelope and, taking her hand once again, to her quivering delight, he gazed longingly into her eyes. "I shall be happy to attend, Miss Tarkington," he said, his voice thick with implied desire to be in her company, and hers alone. Disengaging his hand with apparent regret, he turned to Abigail and Maude. "I look forward to seeing you there, dear ladies." He bowed slightly. "Now, if you will excuse me?" And with no further explanation, he turned and slipped away into the crowd.

Penelope's devastation at his sudden departure was plain for all to see.

"May I get you ladies some punch?" Matthew asked, pretending not to notice his sister's discomfort. Not waiting for a response, thrusting his hat and cane into her hands, he too vanished.

Fussing with Matthew's hat and cane, Penelope's attention was further distracted by trying to locate Bruce's figure among the people that swarmed about in the huge room.

Abigail opened her fan and, placing it in front of her face, motioned for Maude to lean close. "What a bounder!" she whispered, confident that Penelope would not overhear, what with the noise from the myriad conversations that reverberated in the high-ceilinged room.

"Perhaps he only meant to be gracious?" Maude replied, the expression on her face denying her words.

"I do hope you are right." Abigail sighed. "Miss Tarkington seems smitten."

Maude shrugged.

Abigail snapped her fan shut. It galled her to see any woman fret over a man and, casting about for a safe topic to distract Penelope with, she took the opportunity to ask, "How long has Yasushi been in your employ, Miss Tarkington?"

Keeping her gaze upon the crowd in case she might see Bruce again, Penelope replied, "Just a few months." At that moment, turning sideways to slip by some people without disturbing their conversation, Bruce happened to glance in her direction. Instantly her hand was up in a kittenish wave, not a pleasing gesture for someone her size. "Since just before Christmas." Bruce did not seem to see her, and she turned her attention to Abigail. "Why do you ask?"

Ignoring her question, Abigail continued, "Did you check his references?"

"Of course!" Penelope said sharply. "What do you take me for?"

And then it was Abigail's turn to be distracted. Looming beyond Penelope's shoulder, none other than the large William approached dressed in haole clothes. As he towered over them, his face haggard, Abigail thought he resembled someone else, but could not place him. Smiling inwardly, she realized that it was the change from his native garb that caused the feeling of familiarity—it was himself he resembled.

And in the warmth of his charm, she forgot that she had been concerned about how he would receive her when they met again, since he had been less than friendly at the police station. His hat and cane held at the proper angle, he performed all of the formal gestures of greeting as skillfully as any haole gentleman, and had Maude actually smiling with his lilting manner of speaking.

But when he took Abigail's hand, he squeezed it. At first

she was shocked, thinking him to suddenly be another Bruce Dalton, which had not seemed likely while he'd been greeting Penelope and Maude. Yet while his glance was intense, it did not repulse her the way Bruce's had. When he let her hand go there remained a piece of paper in her palm. Eager to read its contents, it was all she could do to slip it into her reticule for later.

"I am sorry about the princess," Penelope said when the formalities were complete.

"Thank you, Miss Tarkington," William replied patiently.

Penelope shrugged.

Turning to Abigail, his gaze was sad as he said, "I understand that you are looking for Princess Lilliana's killer?"

Careful not to look up at him through her lashes like a coquette, Abigail tilted her head so that she could look at him directly as she nodded her assent.

"I am most pleased to hear it," he said politely, as if it were no more than a passing concern. "If there is anything I can do to help, pray do let me know."

Although she was burning to ask him questions on the spot, something told her it would be a mistake to do so, and she trusted that the note would tell her when and where. As he made his excuses and left them, it was her turn to gaze wonderingly after a man.

Penelope touched Abigail's arm. "You know, Miss Danforth," she said upon attracting her attention. "Come to think of it, I did not."

"I beg your pardon?" Abigail asked, completely bewildered.

"You know. Check Yasushi's reference. I tried ringing her up, but the operator said she had gone stateside for the holiday and would not return until after the New Year. I had a large party to arrange for, and with Father taking ill, I just could not wait. And by the time the New Year came Yasushi had proven himself to be so reliable and efficient it seemed pointless."

"Who had recommended him?"

"No one that I know."

"Then how—?"

"He appeared in response to an advertisement I placed in the paper." Penelope stopped her tale for a moment to return a salute from a thin, wraithlike woman in a nearby group. "All very disagreeable."

Although impatient for Penelope to continue, Abigail smiled also. "In what way?" she asked.

"Ah Soy Chan had been with us for many years, but father felt that, what with the plague and all, we should pay more attention to the Chinese Exclusion Act." Penelope paused. Then shrugged. "Well, it was politic to let him go. Yasushi brought a letter with him when he came for an interview."

"So, except for his performance these last few months, you know nothing about him?"

"Why do you ask?"

Abigail looked about significantly, implying that she was unwilling to speak about Matthew's predicament in front of so many eager ears.

Penelope was wide-eyed with astonishment. "But why would Yasushi—?"

Putting fingertips to lips to quiet the large woman, Abigail whispered, "He might be in cahoots with the culprit."

"What shall I do?" Penelope wailed. "My father is ill. I cannot sack him now without an explanation."

"No need," Abigail said soothingly. "Just be certain that your brother takes nothing from him."

Unable to ignore the thin woman's invitation any longer, Penelope moved to join her, gesturing for Abigail and Maude to come along.

Before joining Penelope, Abigail once again resorted to her fan to conceal a few words with Maude. "I wonder if I might prevail upon you to do me a great favor in the morning?" she whispered.

"What might that be?"

"Distract Miss Tarkington somehow—keep her occupied at something."

"Might I ask why?"

"I must take Mr. Tarkington his breakfast tray," Abigail

said. "There is something I must know, and he is the only person who can tell me."

"Oh, my, Miss Danforth," Maude replied quite seriously. "Pray do be careful not to kill him."

Had he been allowed to go to the beach, Kinkade might well have been on vacation. The food was excellent except for the slimy stuff they called poi. Made from pounded taro root, no matter what he stuck in it, including his fingers, it tasted like nothing. After it fermented for a day or two it tingled on the tongue, but still had no taste. Fortunately, fresh fruit abounded and the bananas were the best he'd ever tasted. The cook did something to pig he'd never tasted before, and anything that came wrapped in ti leaves was delicious.

The nights were bad when he lay on his cot in the dark, and with nothing else to occupy his thoughts he would remember why he was in jail. Her smile. How he longed to touch her hair. But the days were more than tolerable. He was allowed outside for exercise, and although watched carefully, he was not cuffed. His captors were a cheerful lot, and after the first few days when he'd grown too bored to remain silent, he'd begun to respond to their friendliness, and had struck up a few conversations. When they discovered how well traveled he was, he became quite popular, especially with the younger officers who had no hope of leaving the islands. With no duties to perform, and pleasant company to while away his time, he did not begrudge Abigail the time it would take to find Princess Lilliana's killer. If she took long enough, he might even learn to like poi.

▽

10

COCK'S CROW AGAIN, AND again Abigail tried to shut out the bird's celebration of the new day with her pillow. And again the stratagem failed. Tableaux from the crowded room at Iolani Palace followed her into the darkness. The reception had been interminable. With the note from William burning a hole in her reticule, fairly aching to read it, she had joined Penelope and the thin woman who turned out to be a wealthy cousin of Bruce Dalton's, a Mrs. Greeley. The ghastly woman had prattled on and on about her fear of the plague, and how the yellow heathens deserved to be burned out, and every last one of them should be shipped back to China so they could not build another such pigsty. When Abigail had ascertained that only six cases of the plague had caused such devastation, it had taken all of her training in the social mores to keep from quitting the palace altogether.

All but fawning over Mrs. Greeley, Penelope added such hate-filled vituperation to the conversation that Abigail could take no more. With a grim-faced nod at Maude, she had turned away intending to escape into the crowd when Matthew had appeared. From the expression on his face, she had surmised that he knew the thin woman and her views, and found them distasteful. Or he might have had his brow furrowed from the effort of holding three glass cups of punch by their handles without spilling. Whatever the source, his grin was sheepish as he apologized for taking so long, hoping that the girls had not suffered overmuch from thirst in his absence.

Abigail was parched, and had taken a rather undignified gulp when she suddenly wondered what Mrs. Greeley would do if she knew that Matthew might be a leper. She choked, imagining the woman jumping straight in the air, screeching like a banshee and, hairpins loose, hat askew, flying out of the room without her boots touching the ground.

Knowing Abigail to have been speechless with anger but a moment ago, a much-puzzled Maude had patted her on the back. She could swear the girl was concealing laughter behind her fit of coughing, and could not imagine what had wrought such a swift change in mood.

A fit of giggles struck Abigail again at the memory, and she was forced to shove the pillow aside to get some air. And face the day.

What to wear? The rooster had awakened every bird and animal in the vicinity, and the resultant cacophony did not aid her concentration. William's note had promised that a carriage would call for her at ten this morning. Since only Jacqueline and Maude knew of her dislike for shopping, the ruse should work nicely for the Tarkingtons. Although they knew she sought the princess's killer, William had pleaded for secrecy. She had decided to trust him; therefore she needed to be suitably attired for the stores.

However, having sensed Mr. Tarkington's penchant for the ladies, she wished to use it to advantage and appear as feminine as possible while serving him his breakfast. Should she manage to engage him in conversation, which was the true purpose of her taking him his tray, she would scarcely have time for Jacqueline to anchor her hat and draw on her gloves and be ready for the carriage. A complete change of clothes was out of the question.

Jacqueline understood her difficulty at once. The morning

suit with braid decorating the bodice of the jacket was called for. All of the blouses that were normally worn with it were too tailored for the serving of the breakfast, but the little genius of a seamstress had the solution. It took her but a twinkling to snip the seams to separate the top from the skirt of the ruffled lace gown she had worn at dinner the night of the rain. With no time to hem it properly, the rough edges would be concealed in the waistband of the suit skirt with no one the wiser. Absent from that dinner, Mr. Tarkington would not recognize it.

"As soon as miss is sitting in the chair, he is seeing nothing but the pretty blouse, no?"

And it had worked exactly as Jacqueline had predicted. Seated beside his bed, where she had been invited—nay, begged—to stay, from his vantage point of sitting upright against his pillows in bed, Abigail's lap, and therefore the tailored skirt, was cast in shadow with only the dainty shirtwaist in view. Jacqueline had taken particular care with the tendrils that escaped her hair and, her color high with anticipation, Abigail was a vision of delicate Victorian womanhood.

Abner was not so well. He had spent a restless night, and felt peevish. The sight of a pretty young girl, not his daughter, had cheered him mightily, and he sipped his tea with some gusto, hoping it might refresh him enough to get the most from her company.

"How are you feeling this morning, sir?" Abigail asked as she watched him pour his second cup.

"God has repossessed my health, Miss Danforth," he said with a sigh. "He has seen fit to keep me alive, but I must admit I am not particularly fond of His decision. I would rather He made up His mind to restore me, or get on with it and call me upstairs." He took a quick sip of tea, but before the cup touched his lips he had a hand in the air to forestall any comment from Abigail. "Or dash me to the other place," he amended with a twinkle in his eye. "Now to what do I owe the honor of your bringing me my breakfast, young lady?"

"Your daughter was otherwise occupied—"

"Now, now, Miss Danforth." Although his glance was admiring, he had a suspicious brow raised. "Houseguests do not act as servants in a servant-filled house. I pay Yasushi handsomely. He might not have liked doing it, but he would not dare refuse."

Abigail was not good at dissembling, a quality she sorely missed in moments such as these, since she had not foreseen his curiosity. Guilty as charged, she blushed as she gazed at her hands in her lap, seeking an answer that would satisfy him.

Forking a chunk of pineapple, he glanced at the blushing girl. "Cat got your tongue, eh?" His grin was mischievous. "Let me guess." He paused, waving the pineapple thoughtfully, as if he were having difficulty coming up with an answer. When he felt he had her full attention, he continued, "I do believe you must have an interest in my son." He popped the pineapple into his mouth, and searched his plate for another.

Abigail had given much thought as to how she was going to broach this subject if given the opportunity, and his health seemed to warrant it. Despairing of having a plan other than to ask him about Luke, although she knew he meant Matthew, she could not resist using this gift of an opening. "Well, yes, sir, that is true—"

"Aha!" he exclaimed triumphantly, spearing another chunk. "It is as I thought!"

"I doubt that, sir—"

"Do not contradict me, girl!" he exclaimed not unkindly. "I can tell young love when I see it!"

Abigail took a deep breath. Before her courage could desert her, she said, "My interest lies in your oldest son."

Abner's fork clattered on the plate. Color drained from his face as he clutched at his chest, staring into space.

For one horrible moment Abigail thought she had killed him. She started to rise from her chair.

"My pills!" he exclaimed, his voice a mere croak. He

waved his free hand in the direction of the nightstand. "My pills, my pills."

A bewildering array of bottles and potions were in a tray under the lamp, along with a pitcher and water glass. Not having the faintest notion which one he needed, Abigail grabbed the first bottle at hand that contained pills rather than liquid. Sitting on the edge of the bed, she held the bottle in front of his face. On the second try she had located the one he sought and, swiftly opening the cap, put one in his outstretched palm. Placing it deep under his tongue, he rested his head against he pillows, shaking it from side to side to refuse the glass of water she held out for him.

Convinced she had nearly cost the old man his life, and thoroughly chastened by her carelessness, Abigail placed the unwanted glass on the nightstand with the pill bottles. She turned toward the door, planning to tiptoe out.

Abner stirred, and held out a hand to her. "I pray you, do not leave, Miss Danforth." His voice was still barely above a croak, but some color had returned to his cheeks.

Much relieved by this sign of recovery, Abigail regained her chair.

"Who told you I had another son?" he asked. "Penelope?"

Knowing nothing about heart conditions, only that common sense told her that shock could not be efficacious, Abigail shrugged, quite willing to give up her quest if it was going to prove that dangerous to him.

"How dare she!" he exclaimed, his color more than fully returned.

"She told me no particulars, sir," Abigail said soothingly, trying to calm him.

"I should hope not!" he exclaimed.

"Matthew said he was twenty years older—"

"Matthew!" He glared at her. "What else did Matthew say?"

"Why nothing, sir," Abigail replied. "He said he would not know his brother if he met him, since they were so far apart in age and that he had no memory of meeting him."

Abigail was ready to ascribe magic to the pill he had placed under his tongue. Whatever it contained had restored him so swiftly that he picked up his abandoned fork. As she watched him tackle his breakfast anew, she waited patiently for him to finish chewing over his thoughts as he chewed his food. Rinsing down the last of his poi-dipped toast with a sip of tea, he turned his gaze upon her. "Why do you want to know about Luke?" he asked.

Had she had any doubts before about Penelope's assessment of her father's ability to hear the truth of Matthew's predicament without a deleterious effect upon his health, she had none now. Unable to hint at her true reason, and with no false one at the ready, she could but shrug lamely and, standing, lean over to remove the tray from his lap. Burdened with the tray, she was halfway to the door when he called out to her to return.

"Put that thing down, and sit by me, girl," he said, his voice gruff.

Not knowing what to expect, but figuring she could outrun him if it came to that, Abigail placed the tray on the foot of the bed and, pulling the chair close, sat, not bothering to align her skirts.

"It would appear that sooner rather than later, I am going to be meeting my Maker, Miss Danforth."

"Oh, sir, surely not—"

"Now, none of that!" he exclaimed. "I receive quite enough of that nonsense from Penelope." He shook his head. "I think I finally understand why the Catholics are so fond of their priests," he said with a wry smile. "Perhaps confession could be good for the soul."

Abigail felt anything she might say would sound frivolous, so she kept her peace and waited for him to continue.

"No one but Luke and I know what happened." He paused. "And to tell the truth, only Luke really knows." He paused again, longer this time, his brow furrowed, his eyes sad.

Again, Abigail bided her time.

Lifting his chin, Abner turned his head and looked directly

at Abigail. "Everyone thinks I disinherited Luke, Miss Danforth," he said. "I do not disabuse them. Even Penelope and Matthew believe so." He shrugged, his smile bitter. "I have allowed them to believe it because it keeps them in line." He sighed.

Although she felt his sentiment cruel, the pain in his eyes was hard to witness, and Abigail lowered her gaze to her hands, which were folded in her lap.

"When Luke's mother died, I put him out to a Hawaiian family. Worst mistake I ever made," he said bitterly. "When he turned fifteen, he had become unmanageable, and I sent him to California to school." His gaze turned inward, toward the past. "Penelope was just three when he came home for that first Christmas. He hated California. He hated the white man's school, the white man's way of doing everything." Abner paused, and cleared his throat. "He hated me."

Reaching for the water on the nightstand, Abner swallowed half a glass before continuing. "I forced him to go back." Raising the glass to his lips, he finished it. Staring at the empty glass, he sighed heavily. "Luke disappeared."

"Disappeared?" Abigail exclaimed. "How is that possible?" she asked, knowing full well just how possible it could be.

"At first I could not believe that he had actually defied me, but when the school wrote asking where he was, I finally realized that he was gone."

"Did the police—?"

Abner held up a hand to forestall her questions. "You will probably find this difficult to understand, Miss Danforth, but I was so angry with him at the time, I did not care what had happened to him. He had made it abundantly clear that he despised everything I stood for—my marriage, my desire to see these islands prosper, even my religion." He waved an accusing finger in the air. "Especially my religion!"

"Then you did not look very hard for him?" she asked, careful to keep her tone free from accusation.

"Only much later," he replied. "When Matthew was born. But then it was much too late. He had vanished without a trace."

"I see," Abigail said, shaking her head solemnly.

"I never have found out what happened."

"To the contrary, sir," Abigail said, surprised that he did not know. "It should be perfectly clear to you what happened."

"I beg your pardon," Abner said with a frown. "What can you mean?"

"If I may say so, sir," Abigail reached out to touch his hand in sympathy, "your son Luke disinherited you."

Despite Jacqueline at the ready with jacket, hat, gloves, fan, parasol, and reticule, and Abigail's dashing about in an un-ladylike haste that would have offended Kinkade's sensibilities had he been witness to it, William's carriage had been waiting some minutes by the time she could gain it.

The driver had dismounted and had been amusing himself by tossing stones at birds in a ginger bush with the yard boy. Immediately upon seeing her hurrying down the steps, he quit their game and, tipping his cap, dusted his hands apologetically before handing Abigail up into the enclosed cabriolet.

Abigail expected William to be in the carriage, and was surprised to find it empty. She scarcely had time to wonder where he'd got to, much less get annoyed at having to wait for him after she had hurried so, when, with a cheerful jingle of the harness, they were off. Breathless and hot from her running about and in need of an airing, Abigail was disappointed that the carriage was enclosed. She would have much preferred one open to a breeze, and she realized that, while the vehicle was common on the streets of London and New York, this was the first such enclosed carriage she had ridden in since she had been on the island. That he chose not to wait within its privacy impressed upon her all the more his seriousness in maintaining secrecy, and she wondered at her wisdom in having told Maude of their tryst.

Her fan, which she used expertly, did little to cool her down, and even less to cool her temper, and the farther they went, the more upset she became. The isinglass windows were spattered, rendering a view from them impossible, and she could not tell where they were going, not that she could have had she been able to see out, since she knew almost nothing about the geography of the island.

At length, she did begin to feel cooler, not from her efforts with her fan, but from a close exposure to a strong breeze from the ocean, which penetrated the cab. The carriage halted, and her suspicion was confirmed when she heard the surf nearby.

But instead of moving on, the carriage door was suddenly opened, and there stood William dressed in nothing more than a loincloth with a breastplate of finely woven feathers to clothe his nakedness. He motioned to her that she could get out instead of his getting into the carriage. She expected rough handling, a grabbing by the elbow, or some such, but he handed her down with but two fingers like any well-bred gentleman.

The stiff breeze from the ocean precluded her opening her parasol, and she noticed that he took care to guide her to the shade under the palms to spare her any exposure to the sun. As much as she chafed at the punctiliousness of those manners imposed upon her, she did appreciate them in a gentleman, especially when so unexpectedly performed by a man garbed in feathers and a loincloth. Since he had gone to such great trouble to seek her out, she further trusted him to speak in his own time and, except for the shy smile bestowed upon their first meeting, she waited for him to open the conversation as if they were in a drawing room instead of on a deserted beach.

For some time he gazed out to sea, the wind playing havoc with his overlong hair in a manner that a haole would have found irritating. At long last, he turned to her, and bending down from his great height so that she could hear him without shouting into the wind, he said, "Princess Lilliana's father will like you, Miss Danforth."

Hand upon her hat to keep it seated, Abigail looked about for someone else. "Her father?" she asked, glancing about, delighted with the opportunity to meet him.

"He is not here," William replied. "He first wished to test your mettle before meeting you."

"My mettle?"

"When I told him about a strange haole wahine with a firm jaw and intelligent eyes who did not flinch upon seeing a huge, half-naked, painted savage attack her servant, he became curious to meet you."

"But why a test?" she asked.

"Fear can destroy anything placed in its path, and if it possessed you, it would be futile for you to meet."

"What test?" Abigail asked. "When does it begin?"

William threw his head back and laughed. When he sobered, he said, "There is no other wahine, haole or Hawaiian, who would have taken my note on faith and climbed into a closed carriage unattended." He waved in the direction of the waiting carriage. "Then, upon having the door opened by such as me, you not only did not scream and shrink away, and order the driver to take you to safety, you joined me on a deserted beach."

Even though she'd had many an argument with Maude concerning this very issue, Abigail did not think her actions unusual for a professional. She looked at him with a blank expression.

"And most important, you did not natter at me with questions, but waited in silence for events to unfold."

Abigail shook her head in puzzlement. "Nothing I did should be considered out of the ordinary."

"Exactly so, Miss Danforth," he said. "That you believe yourself to be ordinary, in the face of your extraordinary behavior, is another reason he will like you."

"I would be honored to meet him," Abigail said, truthfully enough. She hoped none of the concern she felt showed in her demeanor, since the matter of her courage was crucial as she added, "I have been given to understand that he is a kahuna?"

William nodded.

She cleared her throat. "I have also been given to understand that there are two kinds—?"

William threw back his head and laughed.

Annoyed by his response, Abigail said, "Then may I assume that the claim that a kahuna 'ana'ana can pray someone to death is an exaggeration?"

William sobered instantly. "Forgive me, Miss Danforth," he said. "It is no exaggeration. Far from it. It is just that her father is such a great healer and gentle man, that you could even entertain the thought that he might be 'ana'ana is ludicrous." His eyes were serious. "I am deeply impressed that you would be willing to see him before you were certain. He will consider it another example of your courage."

As Abigail regained the carriage, she could not believe that she possessed any courage at all. Knots formed in the pit of her stomach while she contemplated Maude's reaction to her going upon a day-long excursion into the hills alone with him.

▽

11

FOR THE FIRST TIME in her life, Abigail wore the same costume in the afternoon that Jacqueline had put on her in the morning, without changing for lunch, and back again. But there had scarcely been time to change carriages, much less clothes, by the time she got back to the Tarkingtons'.

After leaving William on the beach, loath to ask his driver to stop at Bancroft's just so she would have a parcel to show for her supposed shopping excursion, she had instead indulged in the luxury of sitting all alone in the Elite Ice Cream Parlor, savoring a triple-dip dish of ice cream. The driver had at first demurred, but could not resist her offer to treat him to a cone, which he ate while standing outside by the carriage. Skipping a healthy lunch in favor of a sweet was another first, and should not be repeated or she would soon gain the size of her hostess, she chided herself. She decided to forgo the change in clothes, which would make her late for the call upon Yasushi's former employer.

When she had called for an appointment with Mrs. Herbert, she could have easily asked her about Yasushi over the telephone, and saved herself and Penelope the trip, but she had not wished the nature of her conversation to be broadcast over all of Honolulu by the operators.

She would have preferred to make the call alone, but Penelope had insisted upon joining her. And when Abigail climbed into the Tarkingtons' carriage, a sour-faced Penelope was waiting. The wheels barely began turning before Penelope said, "I do not appreciate your sneaking in to see my father behind my back."

Abigail blushed. "It was not behind your back—"

"All you had to do was tell me you wished an interview and I would have arranged it."

"It was an innocent happenstance," Abigail protested, blushing at the lie. Wishing again she was skilled at the fine art of dissembling, she added, "I just happened to be near the kitchen when Miss Cunningham called you away—"

"I was hard-pressed to explain how you had gained possession of his tray," Penelope interrupted. "What purpose did you have in seeing him?"

Aware of the cruel sword Mr. Tarkington held over her and her brother, Abigail wished she had not given her vow. Sworn to secrecy regarding Luke, she felt it best not to mention his name, which might lead the conversation into a disastrous direction. "I took him his tray, Miss Tarkington," she replied, which was all that remained to say of the truth.

Penelope glared at her. They drove most of a block before her expression softened. "I must thank you for your thoughtfulness." She sighed. "As sick as he is, Father likes to know what goes on under his roof!"

"I understand perfectly." Abigail touched Penelope's arm conspiratorially. "My father is exactly the same."

"And I suppose I must thank you for taking Matthew's part," Penelope said with some reluctance.

With a light smile and nod of acknowledgment, Abigail filed away Penelope's reaction for pondering upon at a later date, and they rode the rest of the way in silence.

However, as the Tarkingtons' driver turned the carriage into the Herberts' street, Abigail could not help but look at Penelope in wonderment. How could it be that such tiny houses could require servants? A yard boy perhaps, and maybe a cook, or a weekly laundress, but a majordomo of Yasushi's qualifications who could manage a staff? Perhaps the neighborhood would improve, she thought. Perhaps they were on the wrong street?

But no. Halfway into the block the driver pulled up to a halt in front of a dwelling that, while it was made of wood, was little more than a shack. Abigail checked the address against the note that Penelope held and had to agree that they were in the right place.

With the driver's assistance, Abigail stepped out of the carriage and waited for Penelope to descend before starting up the grass path to the lanai.

One knock brought a woman to the door carrying a toddler on her hip. From her frazzled appearance she could have used a servant's help.

While Mrs. Herbert was polite enough, she did not invite the two women in, but did indicate that if they chose to sit on the lanai, she would take a minute and join them.

Refusing the rocker, the better for the young mother and her son, Abigail remained standing, wondering at the mother's utter fascination with her child. He was cute enough, to be sure, but could not talk except for a gurgle, and that he could occupy the whole of her attention was a mystery.

Penelope sat on the edge of the only other chair. "We knew we would be in neighborhood," she lied with an ease that Abigail could only wish she possessed. "And since you were not available last December, I thought I might drop by and ask you about Yasushi in person."

Busy smiling at and bouncing the baby on her lap, Mrs. Herbert paid scant attention to Penelope. "Yasushi?" she asked, distractedly.

"Yasushi Miamoto, your Japanese houseman."

Mrs. Herbert glanced briefly at Penelope, her face still smiling at her baby. "What Japanese houseman?" she asked.

Abigail and Penelope exchanged glances.

"Did he not work for you?" Abigail asked.

"I never heard the name before now," Mrs. Herbert replied.

"But this is your telephone number," Penelope said with a puzzled frown. "And this is the correct address—"

"Did you by chance go stateside for Christmas, Mrs. Herbert?" Abigail interrupted.

"Why, yes, we did," she said. "My parents wanted to see their new grandson and sent us passage. How did you know that?"

"When Yasushi answered my ad, he gave your name to me as a reference," Penelope said. "When I telephoned your number, the operator said you had gone stateside."

"Well, that much is correct," Mrs. Herbert replied. "But until this very minute I had never heard the name of Yasushi Miamoto."

"I shall sack him at once!" Penelope exclaimed the moment they gained the privacy of the carriage.

Abigail settled herself stiffly beside the agitated woman. "That would be a capital mistake, Miss Tarkington," she said firmly.

Penelope pulled away, looking at Abigail in disbelief. "But the scoundrel is poisoning my brother!"

"We have no proof whatever that what you say is true," Abigail said, astounded at the woman's leap in logic. "What reason would he have?"

"As you said!" Penelope continued to look at the young detective as if her memory were faulty. "He is working in cahoots with someone else, probably Luke."

"If you discharge him, we will never find out who that person is, now will we?"

The carriage slowed and made the corner before Penelope spoke. "I suppose you are right," she replied grumpily. "How do you propose to find out?"

"I have methods," Abigail replied, not intending to be secretive, but in truth she had no idea what those methods were except to begin by questioning Yasushi.

"Well, I shall have a word with him when we get home,

I'll tell you that!" Penelope grumbled. "Imagine, lying to me like that!"

"I would much prefer that you leave such questions to me, Miss Tarkington."

"He is my servant, Miss Danforth!"

Abigail hesitated. "Perhaps you are right," she replied. Raising a cautionary finger, she added, "But if you should offend him and he should quit, it would be a disaster. He could disappear and we would never find out who employed him."

They rode several blocks in silence before Penelope turned to her. "Might I prevail upon you to tell me what to say?" she asked politely.

"Of course." Abigail softened at once. "Perhaps we could interview him together?"

"I really am in your debt for taking Matthew's part, Miss Danforth," Penelope responded with infinitely more sincerity in her tone than when she had expressed the same sentiments before their interview with Mrs. Herbert. "As you can see, I would have made a dreadful muddle of things."

Pleased by the compliment, Abigail began to feel some rapport with the difficult woman and, taking advantage of the opening, said, "I wonder if you could give me some advice?"

Penelope smiled. "Nothing would please me more, Miss Danforth," she said sincerely.

Abigail moved closer upon the carriage seat, as sisters are wont to do when discussing beaux. "What does one wear to a croquet party?" she asked as if Penelope's answer was the most important thing in the world. And unbeknownst to her, at that moment, it was.

* * *

Once again, Jacqueline came to the rescue. Her genius with corsetry rearranged Penelope's generous figure and, with a few nips and tucks in one of the woman's flowered prints, she appeared to be voluptuous instead of merely heavy. With the judicious use of rats and Abigail's curling irons, she made the most of Penelope's thin hair so that it flattered her face, calling attention to her eyes rather than her chins. The changes were not so drastic as to make Penelope self-conscious, but enough to put a twinkle in her eye. Hat pinned at a saucy angle instead of flat and, with her newfound sparkle, she was actually almost pretty.

That there was a difference there could be no doubt, since Bruce Dalton scarcely left her side the entire evening during the croquet party at the Tibaults', even holding her torch aloft during her turn with the mallet.

In spite of the gossip it was sure to stimulate, Matthew held Abigail's torch. She created a small scandal of her own by removing her gloves to play, but by her third turn they had threatened to split at the seams. She had not played croquet before or she might have thought to bring a second pair. Unlike other ladies who had not, she was unwilling to complete the evening in tatters.

Torn gloves aside, the evening had proved to be more fun than Abigail had had in some time. Being of serious mien, she did not often play games. Conundrums for the most part bored her, and knocking a ball about to get it to go through a hoop would not have appealed to her had she been asked. But the actual swatting of it gave her a keen satisfaction, and when she finished third among the ladies, she was inordinately pleased with herself, and might have played another round had her palms not been so sore.

Watching the torchlight from the sidelines, like fireflies on the expanse of lawn, she did not have to wonder if Mr. Dalton would stick by Penelope if he knew that her brother was even suspected of having leprosy. Careful to keep her tone coquettish, she succeeded in getting Matthew to gossip about his sister and the attentive Mr. Dalton, and discovered that, fourth son of five, Bruce had no money of his own. With the added responsibility of having the large woman's future happiness at stake, Abigail suddenly forgot that she was having fun as her thoughts turned inward.

When she and Penelope had arrived home after their unsuccessful interview with Mrs. Herbert, they had lost no time asking for tea to be served on the lanai off the parlor.

With the intention of making it seem casual, Penelope had allowed Yasushi to almost escape before calling him back to stand before them, arms folded, hands tucked in his sleeves.

His fathomless eyes hid his fear. "I do not write note, miss," he replied truthfully. "I do not—how say—check double if address correct."

"What was the address of your former employer?" Abigail asked.

"I do not remember," he mumbled.

Abigail feigned even more disbelief than she felt as she said, "You reported to work every day for five years and you do not remember?"

Yasushi hung his head, terrified. And angry at this haole wahine with her questions. His mistress had not cared about checking his references, until she had appeared.

"Heathens do not read much, Miss Danforth," Penelope replied. "Nor do they write. It is not necessary. I am not surprised that he does not know."

"I daresay he could lead us there?" Abigail asked, according to plan. She had no desire to press him to do so if it should force him to quit; she had merely wished to watch for his reaction.

"If missy must see," he replied calmly while raging inside, "I show missy."

"That won't be necessary." Penelope dismissed him with a wave of her hand, also according to plan.

Abigail had been disappointed. His expression had been inscrutable.

She'd had an even more difficult time with Maude upon broaching the subject of taking an entire day, to go into the hills with William to meet the princess's father. Alone.

"I cannot permit you to run off into the jungle with that savage!" Maude had exclaimed.

"He is not a savage!" Abigail had replied with some heat. "He is one of the most gentle men I have ever met."

"That is even worse!" Maude was horrified. "You cannot drive off alone with a man, and remain alone with him for an entire day without causing a scandal." She glared at Abigail, arms akimbo. "I simply cannot permit it."

"How else can I interview her father?"

"Very well, I will go with you."

"He sees no one, except by invitation."

"He can come here to meet you!"

"He never leaves the hills."

"Kinkade would write to your father at once!"

"Only if he knew!"

"Can you not see the impropriety—nay—the foolhardiness of your plan?"

"All that you say is true, Miss Cunningham," Abigail agreed with a shrug as she recalled William's comments upon her bravery with irony. It took no courage to trust him enough to see him alone, but it took all of her will to defy the social mores, and risk the good opinion of her friend. "If I am to question an important witness, I have no choice," she insisted. Furthermore, I need your cooperation in providing me with an acceptable excuse for my absence."

In the end, it was Penelope's tenuous position vis-à-vis Bruce Dalton should he discover Matthew's plight that had persuaded the romantic in Maude to relinquish her hold upon her better judgment and not only permit her to go, but to aid her.

With a dose of laudanum in the old man's tea to ensure his sleep, and the other members and guests of the Tarkington household not due back from their croquet party until the wee hours, Yasushi slipped out of the house. Mounting his bicycle, he rode to a hovel on Nuuanu Street. With an opium pipe to calm his nerves for what he was about to do, he engaged one of his young compatriots, skilled in the martial arts, to follow Miss Danforth, whom he described in detail. Should the asks-too-many-questions-haole-wahine place herself in a position wherein an accident might occur with no one the wiser, using his best judgment, he was to provide same.

*   *   *

Waterfalls of purple, red, yellow, blue, orange, and pink blossoms cascaded down the steep cliffs, misting the air with
fragrance. Ferns vied for space, some with fronds wispy as
baby hair, others broad as palm trees. In some spots on the
deeply rutted road, vines were so tangled overhead that they
blocked the sun. Countless birds with feathers brilliant
enough to shame the flowers flitted in and out, singing in
full-throated competition like opera stars at an audition.

Abigail had now been on Oahu long enough to have grown
accustomed to the tumultuous colors and riotous birdsong.
As William turned the one-horse buggy this way and that
up the hill, while she did not permit herself to actually enjoy
the scenery, it no longer offended her, especially since he
knew the names of the birds and flowers in Hawaiian and
Latin as well as pidgin, and regaled her with fanciful stories
about their origins. She was interested to learn that her
Hawaiian name was Apikela.

Responding to his gentle teasing, she laughingly admitted
that if one included the sunsets and moonlight upon the
ocean, Hawaii could be considered beautiful. But paradise?
No. Impossible if one liked snow, which was a concept she
suddenly found difficult to explain. She lost a goodly bit of
credibility when she insisted that an entire lake could freeze
so hard that people could walk upon it. She gave up trying
to describe ice-skating.

Thus engaged upon their journey, and not expecting to be
followed, they paid no attention whatever to the black-clad
Asian mounted upon a donkey who trailed some distance
behind them. The donkey was further burdened with a basket holding several ducks, and had they cast a cursory glance
in his direction, they would have identified the man as being
on his way to either sell them, or to feast. When William
pulled the buggy over so that he and Abigail could disembark
and walk the rest of the way, the man on the donkey was far
enough behind to be hidden from view.

No longer hearing the creak of wheels ahead of him, he

pulled his mount to a halt and, draping the reins over a nearby bush, crept forward to see what was happening. Spying the parked buggy, he decided to follow on foot.

Not too far ahead, the large native-who-must-be-William and the asks-too-many-questions-haole-wahine came upon several dwellings with high-pitched grass roofs in a sun-filled clear space. A muffled rumbling bespoke a nearby waterfall. While various men and women gathered about, all smiling, William greeted a man as large as he with the affection accorded family, then introduced the girl. Surrounded by two large bodyguards, and all those other people, it was going to be impossible to stage an accident. A blow dart, especially in this breeze, would be too fragile since she was gowned in cloth from head to toe, with gloves protecting her hands. A dagger would send everyone searching for the one who had thrown it. Despairing of completing his mission, he made his way back down to the donkey. To wait.

Abigail was much impressed by the princess's father. At first glance, she thought he resembled someone she knew, but concluded that she must be thinking of William. He was a large, well-muscled man with sun-brown skin, but there was something indefinable about him, an almost palpable feeling of power although he wore nothing but a breechclout and a breastplate of feathers and, if one of the humble grass shacks was his home, he possessed none of its trappings. He wore glasses that had dark lenses, a type she had not before seen. Assuming that they protected his eyes from the sun, she thought them clever.

"Come!" he exclaimed, extending a hand toward Abigail so that she would follow him when the introductions were complete. "I will show you the view." Turning away from the group, carrying what might have been a walking stick except that it was too thick, he headed toward an overgrown path. William stayed behind, as did the others. It was clear that the kahuna would be alone with the haole wahine.

Abigail had some difficulty readjusting her eyes to the gloom, and the farther they proceeded up the overgrown path, the more she wondered how the kahuna managed with his dark glasses. But soon they emerged into the bright sun again, and before her lay a scene of such singular beauty that she stopped and stared, transfixed. Across the way a slender stream rushed toward the edge of a cliff and, having no place else to go, plunged straight down. Using the resultant mist as canvas, sunshine painted a rainbow so vibrant that Abigail felt she might touch the colors if she could but extend her hand far enough.

The kahuna unfurled a tapa mat, which she had thought a walking stick, upon a shady spot of grass and invited her to sit. As she settled the skirts of her duster around herself, he joined her, sitting cross-legged. Before she could wonder why he would spoil the sight with dark lenses, he carefully removed them and, with a broad smile, turned to her.

Abigail gasped with astonishment. His eyes were as blue as the sky. "Well, bless my fanny feathers!" she cried, knowing instantly why she had thought he seemed so familiar. "You must be Luke Tarkington!"

12

"HOW DID YOU GUESS!" Luke exclaimed, much impressed. He had not expected her to identify him, intending the removal of his glasses merely as a first step toward revealing his identity.

"I never guess!" she replied testily, offended much like the fictional detective she so admired and wished to emulate. "I observe," she continued. "Although you are—how shall I say—much—ah—rounder?—there is that about your physical build, your chin and nose that resembles your father. However, I must confess, were your eyes brown, your skin color and length of hair would have preserved your incognito." She did not speak of her perception of him as a man of power. Perhaps power was not the right word, she thought, since he also exuded a feeling of serenity, as if he were content with the world as it was, his place in it, and desired nothing. To a man, the powerful men she knew all wanted more of whatever it was they had.

"I had planned to ask that you keep my secret before I revealed myself to you," he replied. "You rather outsmarted me before I could extract a promise."

Abigail drew back in astonishment. "No one on the islands knows you are Luke Tarkington?"

"I would be much surprised if my father knew whether I was alive or dead, much less knew, or cared to know, of my whereabouts. Nor would my sister or brother, since I left long before either was born. My adoptive parents are long dead, and those siblings I was raised with did not know from whence I came. I do not come often to Oahu. When I do, I stay in the hills."

While his command of English was flawless, the inflection he placed upon words rendered his speech exotic to Abigail's ear, and she delighted in his melodic voice. His remarks about his father held a truth that might have been painful, yet his telling betrayed no rancor. But as she gazed at the thin rim of grass that separated the mat upon which they sat from the cliff's edge, she also realized that no matter how well-spoken, he could easily overpower her and toss her down the chasm to be washed out to sea with no one the wiser, his secret safe. She could not believe that he would take the trouble to arrange her visit to do such a thing. However, she did wonder if her investigation into Princess Lilliana's death could be compromised by such a vow.

As if reading her mind, he said, "I will no longer hold you to your promise if it should interfere with finding my daughter's killer."

Suddenly remembering the grief he must be feeling, she reached out to touch his arm in sympathy. "I am so sorry."

Patting her hand, he looked away at the rainbow, and shrugged wordlessly.

"She was called a princess," Abigail said, withdrawing her hand. "As Abner Tarkington's son, you are not Hawaiian royalty—?"

"Her mother was," he replied softly.

"It is amazing to me that no one knows your identity." Abigail shook her head. "In Honolulu, gossip spreads faster than mosquitoes."

"You do not understand the islands, Miss Danforth. Different cultures co-exist here, but they are as separate from one another as fish from birds." He paused. "I never stayed at my father's house. After my last conversation with him, I sailed to Maui to continue my study with the kahunas. I married my princess, and we had Lilliana. I occasionally come here to teach. Maui is my home."

"But your eyes?" she replied. "Did no one in your adoptive family question their unusual color?"

"Hawaiians have a great capacity to accept what is, without delving into details. My new father and mother had been barren, and were happy to have a son. They loved me, and that settled the matter."

"Would no one remember—?"

"I assure you my father changed his friends after he left the church," Luke said. "Anyone who remembered that he'd had a son would assume, if he cared to think upon it at all, that I was dead."

"Does William know you are a Tarkington?"

"No, he does not." He shook his head. "On that you can rely."

Clearly, he preferred the situation as it was since it would be a simple matter to pick up the telephone and change it, or knock upon his father's door for that matter. She had little doubt that the old man would allow him in. If Luke wished it. She hesitated but a moment before trying to find out. "Did you know that your father is seriously ill with a heart condition?" she asked softly.

"It would please me that you not think ill of me, Miss Danforth," he said, his blue eyes gazing directly into hers. "But I am indifferent to the state of my father's health."

"Then there is no hope of a reconciliation?"

"Not even upon his deathbed," he said, his voice expressing regret rather than anger. "Like most good Christians, my father believes that God willed him the earth in the Bible." He smiled ruefully. "With his God-given dominion over everything, he thinks that he has the right to own land, and work his will upon it even if it means the total destruction of an entire people. Father was so busy proving his God is the true one with the right idea, he cast me aside—" Luke held up a hand to forestall her comment as he continued, "which I hasten to add was my good fortune."

"And in the end you cast him aside," she said gently.

"Who told you that?" he asked, his tone sharp for the first time, his gaze piercing.

Abigail returned his gaze calmly. "Your father."

Luke got to his feet in one smooth motion with a surprising grace for one so large. Two steps took him to the very edge of the precipice, and he stood staring out at the view.

Abigail watched him, and in so doing could not help but glance at the rainbow. Expecting it to be diminished, either by a shift in the slant of the sun, or by her eyes having grown accustomed to the colors, she was amazed to see that its brilliance had increased. So engrossed was she by the beauty, she did not notice how long Luke stood there, and was startled by his return.

"The ancients did not believe one could own the earth," he said, crossing his legs after settling on the mat once again. "Neither do modern Hawaiians. My father, and men like him, will eventually destroy these islands with their greed."

"And you mean to stop him?" she asked with raised brow.

"No," Luke replied calmly. "That is impossible." He sighed heavily. "I might as well try to stop the sun from shining."

"What, then?"

"I shall live my allotted time in peace and harmony with the bounty that surrounds me." He smiled, and it was sweet, containing no malice that she could perceive.

But Abigail had already spent more time with him than was usually allotted for a morning call and, concerned that the day was fast slipping away with a long journey ahead, she asked, "I wonder if I might trouble you to tell me why you invited me here to see you?"

He smiled. "William told me about meeting you at the stationhouse," he replied. "You did not flinch when the painted savage threatened your servant," he continued with a wry smile and a twinkle in his eye. "The police will do nothing." He shook his head sadly. "Lilliana was just another disposable native to them."

"But she was royalty—"

"She was not raised to live like royalty." He gestured with his hand to indicate faraway places as he continued, "Schools in Europe, teas at the palace. We kept to the simple ways. The reception at Iolani Palace was more to honor her mother's memory."

"She must have been a girl of immense charm," Abigail said thoughtfully. "Kinkade was apparently smitten at first sight."

He nodded in agreement, and for a moment his eyes grew sad. "I know that finding her killer will not bring her back, but what are your plans for setting your servant free?"

"I confess I have done little, except to ascertain that her death was not an accident." She paused. "I do know that Kinkade had nothing to do with it." She glanced at him swiftly, then looked away before adding, "I have considered William as a suspect."

"William is my son—"

Abigail blushed to the roots of her hair. "In that case—" she began. She stopped, unable to figure out a decent way to say what was bothering her. "That is—if she was your daughter, and he your son—?"

He smiled at her confusion. "William is my son because I took him in as a baby when his own father was killed by sharks," he said, relieving her of the necessity of directly raising the question of incest. "In the old days, had they truly been brother and sister, their union would not have been frowned upon, but blessed. Any baby they might have would have been holy among the holies."

"I see," she said politely, wishing she had not raised the question, or having done so, not left her fan in the buggy so that she could not conceal her flaming cheeks without hiding them in her hands like a ninny.

"Did Matthew tell you that he had been in love with her?" he asked.

"No!" Abigail exclaimed, so surprised that she lost her calm demeanor for the nonce. "Your brother?"

Luke nodded his head in answer.

"Of course, you forbade her to consider it."

"Not at all, Miss Danforth," he said. "My daughter was brought up to follow the dictates of her own heart."

"But Lilliana was his niece!"

"Neither of them knew."

Abigail paused thoughtfully. "How ironic that your daughter had to choose between your adopted son and your brother," Abigail said. "Might I ask how you felt about that?"

"I only wish she were alive to choose, Miss Danforth," he said somberly.

"Pray, forgive my tactlessness," Abigail said, fuming at herself for being insensitive. "I do apologize. I am so intent upon pursuing answers that I quite forget that my questions can wound."

He shrugged as if accepting her apology, but did not immediately respond. "I think there is something you should know, but I hesitate to tell you for fear you will suspect my motives."

"I cannot know what my response will be in advance, sir." Abigail smiled most winsomely. "Now can I?"

He laughed outright. "Well said," he replied. He quickly sobered, before adding, "My daughter spurned Matthew's advances." He smiled ruefully. "She could sense that sugar fascinated him more than she."

It immediately occurred to her that a spurned lover had an excellent reason to kill. At the same moment, it also occurred to her that Luke might prefer to have her think just that, if it would lead her to suspect a brother whose views he held in contempt rather than a much-loved son. She had to admit, however, that what Luke said rang true, since it would give reason for Matthew's uncommon tears. "I see," she said. Deep in thought, she could manage little else.

He gained his feet in that smooth way he had, and held out his hand to assist her.

Abigail took his hand and, although she was standing in a trice, he did not relinquish it. "Hawaiians view a great many things differently than do the missionaries, Miss Danforth," he said, looking deep into her eyes as if asking for an understanding that would not readily be given by most. "My daughter was full of life. She attracted many men. Matthew and Luke were not the only ones. She saw no shame in that. Nor did I." He paused. Sighing heavily, he released her hand. "I grieve for her," he continued. "But may the gods forgive me, perhaps I grieve even more for the loss of my grandchild she carried."

As the Asian descended the path to reach the horse and buggy, a plan for the producing of a splendid accident began to unfold. The beauty of the hills disguised the opportunity for disaster at every turn, the most obvious being an overturned carriage that had been going too fast when it crashed. Better yet, an overturned carriage that had plunged over one of the many precipices that afforded such spectacular views. Or one smashed into the rocky hillside.

Recalling a spot that held both of those calamitous opportunities in one hairpin turn, rather than mount his donkey, he hurried to the site on foot. It was as he had remembered. On one side, the cliff shot straight up from the road, with naked, jagged rocks protruding, unsoftened by the flowered vines that dangled above. On the other, a straight drop down.

Going up the mountain, the curve had not been so dangerous since the going was, of necessity, slow. However, descending would be a different matter, and a prudent driver would slow a buggy to a crawl to negotiate a curve. A timid one would leave the carriage altogether and lead his mount past it. Thrown in either direction, a buggy attached to a runaway horse would meet with disaster, especially if helped by a few rocks in the road. Therefore, a few feet before the curve, he placed some rocks to knock the carriage awry as it rushed downhill. Some deft cuts with his razor-sharp dagger on their horse's flanks and rump would render it skitterish.

Now all he needed was something fail-proof with which to spook the horse just before they reached the curve. Of course, he could jump out into the middle of the path, yelling and screaming and waving his sashband, but, should one of them happen to survive, they might remember him, and know that what had happened was no accident. And then he remembered the ducks.

Matthew's absence from the sugar mill was noted, but he was not missed. The foreman he had replaced when his father had been confined to bed, a man twice Matthew's age, resented the boy's sudden rise in the company, and was glad to have the responsibility of the place to himself again, if only for the day.

Matthew had been careful to leave the house after breakfast as usual, although mounting his gelding without flinching had cost him dear. The pain in his shin was terrible, but ordering a carriage harnessed to take him to work would have caused such speculation that word would surely have reached his father's ear.

Abigail's searching questions about friends and enemies had bothered him mightily. Like most young men of his privileged class, he had lived his life heedlessly, with university an impediment to fun, especially on those days the surf was up. Grades were something one maintained at a level sufficient to avoid a scolding, or worse, a cut in allowance. Golf, canoeing, and racing fine horseflesh vied with surfing for importance, and lastly came girls. Until he had met her.

But then his father had had his first heart attack, and overnight, he'd had to take charge at the mill. He'd ridden the fields since before he could walk, and he was familiar with every step in the refining process, but still he was looked down on as nothing more than the old man's kid. That he had to report to his father every night did nothing to improve the impression, but rather made him into a carrier of tales and, if anything, worsened his position.

Having led a vigorous outdoor life, with a childhood bout of the measles his only memory of illness, when his symptoms had begun, he had ignored them as he had those bumps and scrapes acquired by being active. But everyone on the islands could recite the symptoms of the dreaded *mai paki*, and fear of the disease, and its consequences, had held him hostage until he had finally confessed his predicament to his sister. Much to his relief, she suspected poison. Certainly, believing her had been infinitely easier than facing a truth too terrible to bear.

But Abigail had made him think. He sincerely believed that he had no enemies, yet his symptoms had not abated. So who could be poisoning him? Breaking his solemn promise to his sister, Matthew was on his way to visit a Chinese herbalist to find out the truth.

Penelope could not help herself. Matthew was at the mill, her father napping, and Abigail had disappeared; shopping, Maude said. With Maude ensconced upon a *punee* on the *mauka* lanai absorbed in the latest *Ladies' Home Journal*, it had been too tempting to resist. Waiting until Yasushi went to town for fresh supplies, she slipped into his room for a look around.

The accident unfolded exactly as planned. William handed Abigail into the buggy, whereupon she released the brake before taking her seat. Before climbing in beside her he held the horse by the bridle and walked it around in a tight circle, backing up only once to straighten the buggy's direction, so that it, as well as the horse, faced downhill. Since flies were an ever-present menace and frequently tormented a horse's flanks, he did not notice that it was swinging its tail overmuch. Nor did it seem particularly skittish to him. It had been standing quietly for such a long time, it was probably impatient to get moving, which it did before he was settled in his seat with a firm grip upon the reins.

The first curve in the rutted path was upon them before William was quite prepared, which gave yet another advantage to the Asian as he carefully timed the tossing of the ducks into the path of the oncoming horse.

As they left the Asian's hands, and before they could hit the ground, the ducks spread their wings and flapped them frantically in a desperate, futile attempt to fly out of the way of the horse's hooves. Quacking loudly, the squawking whir of terrified feathers was more than enough to spook the most stable of animals. It completely demoralized William's tormented horse. The panicked animal immediately shot forward, all domestication forgotten in a crazed effort to outrun the shrieking apparitions.

Abigail screamed. Thrown backwards against the seat, she clung to the armrest with one hand and, grabbing the backrest, hung on to it with the other. Knowing that another scream would further excite the horse, she gulped down her fear as the buggy bounded down the rutted road. It hit one hole with such force, her grip was dislodged and she felt her whole body leave the seat before being slammed against it again.

While the horse and buggy took the curves, the Asian dashed in a straight line through the woods, directly to the site of the impending crash to see whether the carriage, and its occupants, plunged down the precipice or smashed into the mountain.

Nothing William did had any effect upon the horse's headlong gallop.

Crouched out of sight, breathless from his run, the Asian raised his fist in celebration as everything happened as he had arranged it. The buggy was going full speed when the right front wheel hit the rocks.

▽

13

The ROCK FLIPPED THE direction of the carriage toward the chasm. Too late, the horse obeyed, veering in the direction of the speeding weight behind him. In a flash, nothing was under its hooves as it left the road and flew into space, pulling the carriage behind. Unable to sustain flight, the hapless animal plunged toward the rocks below, dying instantly upon impact. The carriage was smashed to smithereens.

Pleased with his handiwork, the Asian gained his donkey, and urged it to hurry down the hill so that he could report his success to Yasushi Miamoto.

William knew the road as intimately as the palm of his hand. The knowledge held no comfort. Rather, it filled him with terror as the horse had failed to slow down when he pulled on the reins with all his might. The buggy was going much too fast to apply the brakes, even with his considerable strength. Certain death lay ahead if they remained in the carriage. Better they take a chance upon landing on ferns on the side of the road. A few bruises and broken bones would be a small price to pay for survival.

With no time to spare for the amenities, William grabbed

Abigail by the waist, curling her close to him so that he would absorb most of the impact upon landing.

Instantly realizing what he was doing, Abigail did not recoil from his scandalous breach of conduct but, screams choked off by fear, wrapped both arms around him, unheedful of the fate of her hat.

The oncoming curve, the last before the deadly hairpin, swung wide on the passenger side. While he could not have given it the name of centrifugal force, William instinctively chose the driver's inside curve to jump from, since the other by its very nature added thrust, which would make their landing all the harder. Unbeknownst to them, it had the added benefit of concealing their departure from the carriage from the Asian.

They were airborne but an instant. All too soon the ground rushed up and smacked the breath out of Abigail. It was as well that she had wrapped herself around William so tightly, since he took the brunt of the fall, his back and one elbow losing several layers of skin before they slid to a stop when, his hat lost, his unprotected head struck the root of a tree.

Winded and dazed, Abigail lay in his arms, her eyes shut tight, a scream frozen in her throat, hoping her skirts were in their proper place. Her ankle hurt like blazes, and she prayed that the pain would subside before it became necessary to suffer the unspeakable embarrassment of having to remove her boot to assess the damage.

Matthew could not believe the stink of the tiny shop. It nearly drove him away. From floor to ceiling, every possible nook and cranny had shelves and every shelf was stuffed with all sizes of bottles, tins, boxes, and cartons containing foul-smelling dried, pickled, or preserved powders, liquids, herbs, weeds, potions, and spices that, combined, made the whole unbearable. Underlying the stench was the all-pervasive scent of damp smoke. He held his breath. When compelled to breathe, he did so through his mouth to save the assault upon his nostrils.

Though neither man spoke the other's language, both knew without a word being spoken why Matthew had entered the ancient Chinaman's shop, one of the few that had escaped the fire. Nor was a word exchanged as the old man watched him unwind Penelope's bandage, the better to examine his leg. Matthew also removed his boot so that the ancient one could examine the big toe that had developed a sore, which Matthew hoped had resulted from a misplaced nail in a new pair of shoes.

When the Chinaman first applied the salve to his shin, it stung so badly it brought involuntary tears to his eyes. The pain subsided quickly, and by the time it was bandaged again, his leg was more comfortable than it had been for a week. A dab of the salve on his toe had the same effect.

But wanting above all else a definitive answer to his predicament, did he have *mai paki* or not, the anxious young man were much disappointed with the result, and expense, of his visit. All he could wrest from the Chinaman were vague, thin-lipped shrugs while he carefully measured out herbs that Matthew was to brew into tea. And return in a week.

Now Matthew was left with the problem of how to tell Penelope how he happened to have a different ointment under a different bandage from the one she had put on him, and where to brew the tea, which would no doubt stink to high heaven.

Further, and more seriously, although he had revealed nothing about his identify, he now had to worry if he had placed himself in the position of being blackmailed.

Yasushi's life had been a difficult one, but this day, waiting for his compatriot to bring word of the questioning one's fate, had been one of the worse he had ever spent. He was not by nature a violent man, and regretted what he'd had to do, but she had brought it upon herself with her questions.

It was well after the noon meal, shopping done, the house napping, when at long last he spied his cohort mounted on the donkey, poking toward the house. He rushed outside to be at the gate when he passed, ostensibly to buy a duck if anyone was watching and wondered why they were talking.

Pleased with himself, and wishing to impress Yasushi with his patience and the cleverness of his plan, the young Asian relished the detailing of his triumph.

Eager to hear the fate of the questioning one so that he could return to the house before he was missed, Yasushi tried to hurry him, to no avail. He was horrified upon learning that an innocent man had perished with her, and made his displeasure known in no uncertain terms. It was with a heavy heart that he hurried back into the house.

Abigail opened her eyes, and instantly regretted it. Birds chirruped, insects buzzed, shafts of sunlight penetrated the thicket. Landing in the bed of the softer ferns could not have been more fortuitous. But if another human being saw her at that moment in the compromising position of lying in a young man's arms, be he native or white, alone in the jungle with her skirts every which way, she would be ostracized by polite society, her reputation shattered beyond repair, and all hope of a career that depended upon her good name ruined. And rightly so. Defying convention to pursue a criminal might justify some peccadilloes, but even she knew there were limits, and she had clearly exceeded them all. That her predicament was the result of an accident mattered not a whit.

Blushing furiously, she disengaged herself and sat bolt upright. Her hat was badly askew, and the net tied under her chin securing it in place threatened to choke her. Fumbling with a furious haste, which merely served to make her inept, she found the ends, and pulled. Taking as deep a breath as her corset would allow, she reanchored her hat by feel. As she did so, she looked around, not knowing whether she hoped that no one was about to witness her shame, or if someone would appear to give them a ride down the hill. A bit shocky from the accident, so intent was she upon getting out of the untenable situation of the moment, it did not cross her mind that she had just narrowly escaped death. Or that William might be seriously injured. Or that he had saved her life. Desiring nothing more than to flee, she tried to stand. It was a mistake. She gasped with pain. And sat.

William moaned. "Are you all right, Miss Danforth?" he asked groggily. Not daring to rise, he rubbed his head while remaining flat. His elbow and back stung mightily.

"Yes, quite!" she exclaimed, although she was not at all certain she spoke the truth, since her ankle throbbed alarmingly. Thinking only of escape, she continued earnestly, "We really must be going."

William sat up at once. His head pounding, he cast about for his hat. While he was well schooled in the haole manners that Abigail had found so engaging, men and women had a much freer time of it with one another in his culture, and he was therefore oblivious to her dilemma. He interpreted her behavior as another example of courage. But he now felt the trait unfeminine, and offensive. He was well aware that they had narrowly escaped death. Any Hawaiian wahine, especially his beloved Lilliana, would be clinging to him for comfort, thanking him profusely for saving her life. While he wanted no medal, he did expect some expression of gratitude, and Abigail's aloofness, combined with her strange stories of water hard enough to walk upon that had nothing to do with the miracle of Jesus, convinced him that he would like to deposit her at the Tarkingtons' with all due speed. If anyone could find Lilliana's killer, she probably could, but he wished to play no further part in her attempt to do so.

He heaved himself to his feet with an effort. Tottering for a moment, he waited for his balance to return before warily holding out his hand.

Her ankle too unreliable for Abigail to have any choice other than to accept the offered assistance, she reluctantly reached up. Placing her weight upon her foot, she willed herself to stand despite the pain. Determined to quit the place, and thereafter the young man, as soon as possible, preferably to never see him again, lips thin with the effort not to cry out, she held on to his arm. After a few steps, although she winced with discomfort, her ankle held her weight without collapsing. By the time they found William's hat a few feet down the road, she could walk unassisted and did so.

Both were concentrating so intently upon restoring their clothing to a presentableness that would pass a cursory muster by strangers without causing undue comment, that they walked past the rocks in the road without giving them notice. As they stood at the spot where carriage tracks left the road and stared down the abyss, Abigail extracted a promise from the Hawaiian not to speak of her participation in the accident to anyone of her acquaintance.

Thinking her daft, he nonetheless agreed to say that the loss of his horse and carriage occurred after he put her in a hack for the ride home. Duck farms were ubiquitous upon Oahu, notwithstanding the efforts of some upstanding citizens to control the resultant stench and health hazards with zoning ordinances. Two squabbling birds in the middle of the road was an all too frequent occurrence; therefore, there was no reason for either of them to suspect that the spooking of their horse had been anything but an accident. And so they descended the hill until they came upon a house with a telephone.

The sun was setting by the time an exhausted Abigail arrived at the Tarkingtons' in a hired hack, and hurried into the house with scarcely time to change for dinner.

Busy organizing the meal in the back of the house, and there being no locks on the front door and therefore no necessity for a bell to be rung for someone to enter, Yasushi missed Abigail's entrance. Nor did he keep track of Jacqueline's whereabouts and did not notice when she disappeared to help her mistress dress. The household was abuzz. The master was feeling well enough to dine at the table, and the Japanese was curious about how long they would delay the meal for the questioning one's arrival. Mr. Tarkington's favorite soufflé was on the menu, and he was sorely tempted to tell cook to hold off on putting it in the oven. He had to remind himself to set a place for her.

One look at her mistress's face and Jacqueline swallowed all of her questions about the appalling condition of her clothes. Perhaps she would find out where the grass stains came from if she could arrange to be in the room when Abigail told Maude of her misadventure. She had no doubt that something terrible had happened, nor had she any doubt that her mistress would confide in her friend. But she barely had a chance to mention that Mr. Tarkington was expected to join them for dinner before Abigail silenced her with a glare. Which was probably just as well, since her hairdo was beyond salvaging and had to be taken down, brushed, and repinned. Although Jacqueline noticed and thought it odd that Abigail was not changing boots, because they were in such a hurry, and because Abigail seemed so impatient, she did not comment, or protest.

All Abigail wanted to do was fling herself upon the bed, pull the covers over her head, and have a good cry, a not unreasonable response to what she had been through. However, she would not permit herself to succumb to such feminine weakness, although it cost her dear to maintain her composure. The pain in her ankle had subsided during the carriage ride, but had returned full force when she put her weight on it to walk into the house without limping. Now it throbbed so badly that she was afraid to change boots for fear it would quickly swell so that she could not put on another pair. It would be a nuisance to watch her skirts all evening when she sat so that they hid the toes, but there was nothing for it. In her dazed state, it was all she could do to plan an excuse to escape the inevitable after-dinner entertainment.

On those occasions when guests were invited for dinner, everyone forgathered on the *makai* lanai for drinks, and

Yasushi would announce dinner to the assemblage. When just members of the household had to be assembled, he struck a brass dinner gong with a padded mallet. As children, Penelope, and then Matthew, had taken much delight in enthusiastically thwacking the dinner gong until scolded into doing it properly. Matthew still got a kick out of calling dinner, and tonight he preempted Yasushi's duty while the Japanese put the finishing touches on a huge tray bearing crystal bowls containing artistically arranged fruits.

The final echoes of the gong had faded as Yasushi hesitated in the doorway that led from the kitchen to the dining room, expecting to be told to return the tray to the kitchen to await Miss Danforth's arrival.

And as he counted the inhabitants of the dining room, it would seem that she was indeed missing. Mr. Tarkington had just finished seating Maude to his left and was standing by his place at the head of the table, while Matthew helped his sister to her chair, when a ghost of the questioning one appeared in the opposite doorway. Yasushi gasped.

Smiling gamely, apologizing profusely for being late, Abigail strode briskly to the chair that a smiling Mr. Tarkington was holding for her to his right.

Yasushi lost his grip upon the heavy tray. It fell to the tapa mats with a resounding crash. Crystal bowls worth more than a month's pay each shattered, spilling their contents. In shock, red-faced with shame, he stood frozen, surrounded by shards of glass mixed with fruit and their juices, bracing himself for the inevitable scolding.

Abigail laughed and began to clap. It was, of course, customary to ignore such mishaps in one's own home and pretend that nothing untoward was happening so that the diners' digestion would not be disturbed by any display of anger or displeasure. Naturally, the same behavior was expected of guests, but Abigail could not contain herself. This was no dribbled wine by a careless steward, but the largest mess she had ever witnessed, and she thought it hilarious.

She had been squelching so many feelings, there simply was no more room for another. Her laughter infected the entire table.

Enraged, Yasushi picked up the tray and fled to the kitchen to summon help. Although Abigail's laughter had saved him from a much-deserved scolding, and possibly from getting fired upon the spot, her ridicule was beyond bearing.

The scullery suffered not a few bloody fingers cleaning up the mess, first clearing a path in the doorway so that Yasushi could return with the soup course.

While not actively serving diner, Yasushi stationed himself just outside the door and listened intently. It had not been unusual to hear stories of spills from polo ponies described in minute detail. Surely an accident of the magnitude that she had suffered would be an irresistible topic of conversation.

Not one word.

He began to worry if not one, but two innocent people had been killed. The rest of the evening was an agony of waiting until the household was asleep so that he could sneak out and confront his lying cohort.

Mr. Tarkington retired after dessert, refusing Penelope's offer to read to him. If Abigail had also retired, that would have left Maude, Penelope, and Matthew to play three-handed whist, a most unsatisfactory pursuit. Unable to refuse being a fourth without being a spoilsport and rousing Maude's curiosity, she endured two full rubbers before begging off, pleased with herself for having lasted the evening with no one the wiser about the sorry state of her ankle.

But when Jacqueline pulled off her boot, the jig was up.

"Mon dieu!" the diminutive maid exclaimed. "What happened, miss?" Even through Abigail's stockings, she could see the angry bruise that covered her instep and circled her ankle.

"I stepped in a pothole," Abigail replied, a not unlikely

story since it was rumored that the unwary could fall into one of Honolulu's mud-covered potholes and disappear, hat and all.

"You need the liniment, miss," Jacqueline cried, and before Abigail could protest, she had quit the room in search of the mistress of the house.

Abigail had changed into her nightgown and dressing gown, and had nearly finished braiding her hair, by the time Jacqueline returned bearing a tray with bandages and several jars.

Penelope had insisted upon coming with her. Persuading Abigail to lie on the bed, with Jacqueline hovering nearby, she sat beside her, touching Abigail's ankle gingerly to assess the damage. Declaring it nothing more serious than a nasty bruise, and possibly a strain, she applied a soothing arnica ointment and wrapped it expertly in a bandage. Having found nothing useful in Yasushi's room with which to incriminate him, even though she now had the opportunity to confide in the young detective, the large woman decided not to confess her failure.

Thanking her hostess profusely, Abigail remained in bed, mosquito netting in place, as they let themselves out of the room. Exhausted, relieved that her ankle was not broken, the moment the door closed behind them, she fell asleep.

The argument raged for an hour. Not unskilled in the martial arts, Yasushi was sorely tempted to let fly with a kick or two of his own, but confined his retaliation to words, albeit insulting ones, delivered in a loud and angry voice. He had great difficulty convincing Shin that the questioning one lived. It had been bad enough to have one innocent man's death upon his conscience; Yasushi was now beside himself with horror that he might have caused the death of two people who meant him no harm.

Much red-faced screaming transpired between them before they reached an agreement upon what Abigail had been wearing and therefore certainty regarding her identity. By the time they were both hoarse, they had figured out that the pair must have jumped before the carriage had plunged off the cliff. That she had not mentioned one word of her ordeal at dinner mystified them both.

"She outfoxed you!" Yasushi exclaimed contemptuously.

"A man rescued her," Shin replied, saving face with a philosophical shrug. "Next time she is alone, yes?"

A shared opium pipe quieted their nerves while they made another plan.

$\triangledown$

14

ABIGAIL OPENED HER EYES, instantly awake. For one horrible moment she feared she was lying upon the ferns in William's arms. It was so dark she could not tell if her eyes were open, and only the buzzing of insects reassured her that her hearing was intact. Cheeks hot with embarrassment, she tried to figure out what had awakened her. No loud sound repeated itself. Cautiously, she wiggled her ankle. It seemed fine, if a bit tender, a miraculous recovery considering the pain she had been suffering before Penelope had dressed it.

A large yawn, covered daintily with her hand even though she was alone in the dark, an equally large stretch, which disclosed some stiffness from the fall that she'd not been aware of, and she closed her eyes, fully expecting to fall asleep again. Instead, the questions that had been shoved aside by the shock of the accident and the attendant necessity of keeping it a secret nattered at her, keeping her awake more effectively than any rooster.

If Luke was not poisoning Matthew, who then? Who was Yasushi in cahoots with, if not Luke? Who would have a motive? Unless Matthew was poisoning himself, only Penelope was left close to home, but to suspect her was absurd, since she stood to lose everything. Every question bred a dozen others. Not one had an answer.

And as to the matter of freeing Kinkade, the discovery of Princess Lilliana's being with child was too embarrassing to talk about even in the dark. Pulling the sheet to her chin, as she stared into the blackness she finally admitted to herself that the accident had had little to do with her not bracing William with whether he was the father. Squirming under the covers, she wondered if she could ever summon enough gumption to question a man upon a delicate matter. She had already had enough experience to know that people lied no matter how skillfully a question was put. Nonetheless, questions must be asked. Answers must be had. Even lies sometimes led to the truth if one persisted. But if she was unable to bring herself to ask something just because it flaunted decorum, or offended a missionary, how could she ever hope to be a detective?

Exhausted from the futility of it all, she slid into a deep sleep just as the rooster let go his first squawk. She heard nothing until Maude pulled aside the mosquito netting to serve her tea.

"Come, come, Miss Danforth," Maude said with an unusually cheery smile. "It is time to get up. You are sleeping the day away."

Abigail groaned. Turning over, she opened one eye and peered at Maude. "What are you doing here?" she grumbled. Sitting up, she smacked the pillows and leaned against them. "Where is Jacqueline?" she asked, taking the proffered cup of tea.

"At church," Maude replied. "Afterward she is going to visit Kinkade."

Abigail was about to take a sip of tea, but replaced the cup in its saucer. "Who gave her permission, pray?"

"She tried to wake you twice, Miss Danforth," Maude replied. "When you did not respond, she gave your excuses to the Tarkingtons for missing services. I did not think you would mind rewarding her with some extra time." Maude turned to go. "I had to plead a headache."

"I say, Miss Cunningham," Abigail held out her free hand to stop her companion from leaving, "I wonder if I might ask you a question without divulging the particulars?"

Although they had spent time in one another's company the night before, little real communication had passed between them. Abigail seldom sought her advice, and Maude was curious. "Of course you may." Moving the net aside, she sat sideways on the bed, facing Abigail.

"You are much more clever about matters of the heart than I," Abigail said, taking a deliberate sip of tea.

Maude took it for granted that Abigail was stating a fact, and not merely being modest. She shrugged off the compliment.

Unable to look directly at Maude, Abigail kept her gaze upon her teacup as if her fortune might be found inside. "Would a girl who is—that is—would a girl who found herself in the family way necessarily tell the father?"

Maude looked at her with raised brow, dying to know who Abigail was referring to, hoping she would volunteer the information.

Abigail blushed furiously. She was unclear about the details of the marriage bed, and while she was certain there was more to it, she was also just as certain she had come perilously close to starting a baby herself by lying so close to William. Alone. Maude's penetrating gaze seemed to guess at her guilty secret. She tried to hide her embarrassment with another sip of tea.

When silence did not work, Maude tried another of Abigail's interlocutory tricks. "Had Princess Lilliana lain with more than one man?" she asked, guessing that Abigail was referring to the princess since it seemed highly unlikely she meant Penelope.

Abigail knew that Maude was fishing by referring to the princess by name. Deciding not to deny it, she smiled suggestively, and shrugged her answer.

"The police did not know," Maude said, shaking her head in wonderment. "How did you find out?"

Realizing that Maude would need to know about Luke Tarkington if she was going to be of any real help, swearing her to secrecy upon pain of death, Abigail told her everything. Except about the accident. During the telling, with Maude tying Abigail's corset while asking questions of her own, Abigail managed to dress herself. Her hair was less than perfect, but it would do for lunch since the senior Mr. Tarkington would not be at table.

Abigail was not the only one who had spent a sleepless night. Half dead on his feet from lack of sleep, Yasushi was tempted to stay in the kitchen and snooze in a chair while the busboy served lunch. He and Shin had spent most of the night working out the perfect plan. Bribe driver. Carriage leaves her at secret spot. Poison dart. If she does not fall, push her over cliff. Gone. Simple.

But though he stayed awake the rest of the night, he was unable to figure out how to lure her away from the protection of the Tarkington family and her friends. Hoping against hope that as they discussed the day's plans a solution would present itself, he forced himself to serve the meal. His diligence was rewarded.

The questioning one had accepted the young master's invitation to view the Tarkingtons' fields on horseback the next afternoon. Miss Cunningham had already committed herself to accompany Mistress Penelope to tea at the Tibaults'; therefore the *luna* would ride with them. Perfect. A properly timed telephone message for young master to attend an emergency at the mill before they could ride to the fields, and the rest was easy.

The telephone was in the center hallway where, sooner or later, everyone passed. Matthew had dashed off to the mill in answer to his call, having promised to return for Abigail as soon as possible. Yasushi had only to station himself nearby and wait for her to cross from her rooms toward the stables after she had dressed to wait for Matthew to pick her up.

At long last he heard Abigail approach, but before she was in sight, he picked up the receiver. "Yes, sir," he said loudly when he was sure Abigail was within earshot. "Yes, sir, I tell missy." Even though he deliberately kept his back toward her, the rustle of her skirts betrayed her nearness. Timing it precisely, he turned and pretended to see her just as he dropped the receiver into its cradle.

"Oh, missy!" he exclaimed, feigning surprise. "I no find you when telephone ring. Master Tarkington say he sorry he not pick you. Carriage come take you him, yes?"

"We will not be riding?" Abigail had looked forward to the exercise and was disappointed. And completely taken in.

Yasushi shook his head. "No horse, no horse." He smiled. "Master Tarkington, he send carriage."

"In that case, pray tell the boy to unsaddle Crosspatches," she said, wondering whether to change from her riding costume to something more feminine. But since she had already selected a parasol with ruffles frilly enough for a party, she decided against it.

Shin did not intend to fail a second time. He took the precaution of dipping the razor-sharp points of his ninja star in poison so that it need not make a serious wound. A pinprick would do. It would simply take longer for her to die. He placed the poisoned star in its protective pouch with great care. Tucking the pouch into his sash, he began the journey to his rendezvous with the questioning one.

Abigail had, by now, traveled a goodly bit around Oahu, but once off the paved streets in the middle of Honolulu, most roads resembled little more than dirt paths hewn from the undergrowth, barely wide enough to accommodate a carriage, and it all looked alike to her. Sooner or later, once into the hills, the landscape of mountain rising on one side and sheer drop on the other was a familiar sight. With houses built well off the road, it was impossible for her to tell whether she was in a residential area, on the way to see a particularly spectacular view, or upon a road built for the convenience of hikers that would peter out, leaving her nowhere.

Nor was she alarmed that Matthew was not waiting for her when the carriage rolled to a final stop. The driver would accept neither fee nor tip, further convincing her that he had indeed engaged it for her convenience. She did, however, expect to see cane fields spread below, since they were presumably meeting in this spot to inspect them. While the driver maneuvered the horse around in a tight turn to face it and the carriage downhill, she went to the cliff's edge for a preview.

Shin could scarcely believe how easily everything was unfolding. Well hidden in the underbrush, crouched upon a slight rise before the landscape shot straight up again to form the side of the mountain, he could watch her every move.

As she peered over the edge on the other side of the road, she was in the perfect position for a strike, but the carriage was in the way. While the driver had been well paid for his part in delivering her to this deserted spot, he and Yasushi had agreed that the man should have no further knowledge of what transpired. There was sure to be a hue and cry when it was discovered that she was missing, and the fewer who knew her fate, the better. He assured himself that if she had placed herself in such a perfect position once, she would do so again. Or it would be an easy matter to force her back into it if she moved too far before the driver was out of sight. Thus he was content to wait.

The sun was bright overhead, and although there was a brisk wind blowing that kept the air cool, and made the job of holding a parasol steady a shaky business, she nonetheless opened it to protect her skin from its harsh rays. Expecting to see cane fields spread before her, Abigail was disappointed when there was none to be seen below, but still not suspicious. The driver had gained his seat upon the carriage, and was already too far down the hill to hear her cry should it occur to her to be concerned. Thinking that she might see the cane fields from a better vantage point beyond the cliff side, she started up the road.

Shin was delighted with her move. It brought her closer still. Taking careful aim, he made himself wait until she drew directly in front of him. With a well-practiced flick of his wrist, he threw the poisoned ninja star.

The blustery wind save Abigail's life. A sudden gust caught at her parasol, swerving it into the path of the on-coming missile. The star easily tore through the silk, but one of the struts on the inside further deflected it, and it landed with a harmless clink upon the rocks at her feet.

The shock of its impact upon the umbrella caused Abigail to drop it and, caught in the wind, it began to twirl down the path.

Having learned his lesson about gloating prematurely, rather than running the moment he released the star, Shin had stayed to personally toss her off the cliff in case she did not fall. Stunned by the unfortunate outcome, he was forced to make another plan upon the spot, since it had never oc-curred to him that he might miss from so close a vantage point. It was with contempt that he stared at the bewildered girl, her midsection exposed. A worthy opponent would have been on guard. But now her back was to the high side of the cliff. He would first need to force her closer to the drop before he could shove her off. And for that, he needed to kick her. The thought of actually having to touch her while she lived filled him with disgust, but he nonetheless crouched to jump.

Thinking that a fallen rock from the cliff side had wrested the sunshade from her grip, and wishing to protect her head from another, at the very instant Shin launched himself from above, Abigail bolted for the spot where she'd been standing to chase after the parasol.

Shin landed upon the road in the exact spot he had in-tended, but to no avail. She was no longer near enough to kick.

Abigail was stooped, her hand upon the handle of the

parasol, when she heard a grunt and thud behind her as his feet hit the road. Parasol in hand, she whirled around to see a black-robed Asian crouched to attack her. Stunned by the sight, for the first time she realized she was in danger. Shame washed through her for her stupidity in not having realized that she was being set up.

Having lost the advantage of her not knowing he was there bothered Shin not a whit. Attacking blind was an assassin's work. He preferred a fight. Not that the girl could be called an opponent, but at least she now faced him knowingly. Further, she was now in the right position, away from the protection of the high side of the cliff. All he needed to do was throw her off balance with a turn kick to the stomach, then shove.

In a blur of movement too fast for Abigail to take note of, he took one lunging step toward her. His foot landed in her midsection. It knocked the scream out of her. She fell to her knees, dropping the parasol in front of her.

Accustomed as he was to sparring with other Asian males, Shin knew nothing of corsets. Her steel stays broke his toes, sending a shock wave of pain up his leg when he came down upon his foot to restore his balance from the completed middle kick. The pain so surprised him, he staggered back a few steps.

Nor had the blow doubled her over as intended. Her corset would not permit it. On her knees, she was anchored to the ground too firmly to simply push over the edge. All of his training was for naught as anger surged through him. The maddening, elusive girl must be destroyed as vengeance for the pain she had inflicted. He decided upon a spinning kick to the back of her head, using the heel of his injured foot to knock her out. With a cry coming deep inside his throat, knees bent, steeling himself against feeling pain when his foot struck her head, he propelled himself into the air.

Unable to draw breath from the blow, unable to bend because of her corset, knowing it to be stupid and useless, in a desperate effort to protect herself, Abigail swooped up the silk cover of the upended parasol, tossing it over her head, and fell flat. The parasol spun straight up, handle side out.

Shin's heel struck where Abigail's head had been, but instead of meeting skull, it landed on the inside of the parasol. As his momentum forced it to the ground next to the terrified girl, the struts holding it open could not withstand the impact of his weight, and broke off inside his already injured foot. Shrieking with pain, he stretched his leg wide in an effort to place his other foot upon the ground free from entanglement. In so doing, he straddled the handle. It entered his scrotum as his good foot hit the path.

Abigail hugged the ground, her eyes shut tight.

Screaming in agony, Shin no longer knew she existed. Grabbing the handle with both hands, he spun out of control, trying to pull the parasol free. Unaware that he was even close to the cliff's edge, he lost his balance, and plunged over the side.

Abigail dissolved in tears.

Matthew could not understand it. The house was empty. His sister and Miss Cunningham were presumably at the Tibaults', that was to be expected. A silent peering into his father's room proved him to be napping, also expected. But Abigail was nowhere to be found, nor was Yasushi. And no Jacqueline. Nor was Crosspatches in the stable. The yard boy knew nothing. Standing on the front lanai, he absent-mindedly tapped his thigh with his crop, wondering what to do. Was he that late that he had ridden off somewhere else without him? Pulling his watch from its pocket, he flicked it open. He'd been on time to the minute. He frowned, returning the watch. Not knowing what else to do, he reclined on a *punee* to wait.

Abigail's tears were short-lived. Her attacker's screams had no sooner stopped than she forced herself to sit upright. Choking back the sobs, she searched in her reticule for a handkerchief, and dried her eyes. Even as she blew her nose, she looked around her to see if the Asian had had a companion. She saw no one, but neither had she seen her attacker when she had first arrived, and she was not reassured. Her heart thumping wildly, she ignored the pain in her ribs as she scrambled to her feet. So badly shaken was she that she had to stand still for a moment to gain her balance. Her hands flew to her hat, which with the help of netting securing it under her chin, seemed to have survived. Her parasol was nowhere to be seen, and in the interest of speed, she decided to abandon it.

Knowing that it would be hopeless to try to restore her duster to any semblance of order, she nonetheless brushed at it with her hands as she began the long trek down the hill. At least this time she would have no need to lie to Maude or to her maid about the sorry state of her clothes. She found herself being almost grateful for the experience of the accident, since she had learned that it was more than likely she would find a house not far from the road, equipped with a telephone, and friendly inhabitants only too willing to allow her to use it to call a hack. And the police.

It was not until she was knocking on the door of just such a dwelling that she began to suspect that the accident with William might have been a deliberate attempt upon her life. By the time the driver entered the Tarkingtons' driveway, she was convinced of it. Certain that Yasushi was instrumental in setting her up, and reluctant to be in the house alone with him, she was most relieved to see Matthew hurrying down the steps to greet her and pay the driver.

"Where have you been, Miss Danforth?" he cried as he handed her down.

"Yasushi told me you had called and were sending a carriage." Abigail ignored her aching midsection as she held her skirts to mount the steps.

"Not I!" he exclaimed, grasping her elbow to assist her.

"When the carriage left, someone tried to kill me."

"Miss Danforth!"

Frowning, she held her fingertips to her lips, a signal to

lower his voice. "I daresay he has disappeared?" she whispered, stopping at the top of the steps.

"Quite the contrary," Matthew replied. "I have just sent him off to fetch me some lemonade."

"Capital!" Abigail exclaimed. "We are about to discover who is poisoning you!" And with that she dashed ahead of him to settle herself in the wicker chair that was concealed by potted palms from direct view of the door to the house.

Matthew scarcely had time to recline upon the *punee* before Yasushi appeared in the doorway carrying a tray laden with a pitcher, an ice-filled glass, a bowl of fruit, and plate of cookies. He started toward Matthew.

"I pray you," Abigail said in her most sepulchral tones as he placed the tray on a table in front of the *punee*, "might I have a glass as well?"

Yasushi whirled around toward the voice. Despite his best efforts at remaining calm, all color drained from his face. He trembled with fear, certain he was seeing a ghost.

Matthew had seen enough. "You fiend!" he cried, leaping from the *punee*, hands outstretched to grab him.

Yasushi turned upon his heel and had reached the steps before Matthew could get past the table that stood between them. He all but flew down them.

Matthew followed close behind.

"Be careful!" Abigail shouted as, skirts ankle high, she too dashed down the steps. "He might have a knife!"

Yasushi was agile, and fast, and might have outrun a lesser man, but he was no match for the athletic Matthew, who brought him down with a tackle before he could reach the gate. Both men were sprawled in the dust as Abigail caught up.

Yasushi's silk cap had been knocked off in the fray and, having thought him to be a younger man, Abigail was startled to note he was bald in front. She was even more amazed when Matthew hauled him to his feet. A braid unfolded from the back of his head, long enough to reach his waist.

"Oh, my God!" Matthew exclaimed in disgust, loosening his grip. "You are Chinese!"

"Aiiii, aiiii!" Yasushi wailed. "I am good servant!" He dropped to his knees. "I need job!" he cried. Hands clasped together, he rocked back and forth. "I work hard!"

"Has he been wearing a wig to make him look Japanese?" Abigail asked, by turns amazed and disappointed by this turn of events.

"Exactly so, Miss Danforth," Matthew said. "It is not uncommon. Stories of such deceptions have been reported in the newspapers. Had I not been so preoccupied with other matters, I might have suspected the truth when his references failed to check."

"Then he had nothing to do with poisoning you," Abigail cried. "He was just trying to keep his job. I must have terrified him with my questions."

Listening intently while groveling at their feet, Yasushi, or Ming How Choy as he was known in Chinatown, waited for an opportunity to escape. He had little hope of outrunning the younger, stronger man, but as sole support of his large family, he had to try. The couple hovering above him seemed intent upon their conversation and, taking a deep breath, he sprang to his feet and made a dash for freedom. Before Matthew could give chase, Abigail grabbed his arm. "No," she said, holding fast. "Let him go."

"But he tried to have you killed!" Matthew exclaimed, looking at her in amazement.

"He did not succeed." Abigail shuddered, recalling the screams of the Chinaman as he had fallen over the precipice. Heart heavy, she watched Yasushi, queue bouncing down his back, grow smaller. All of her theories regarding Matthew's predicament were disappearing with him. She had no idea how to begin anew. Her midsection, and ankle, began to ache in earnest.

$\triangledown$

15

Matthew stared after the fast-disappearing China-man. Slowly, he turned to look down at Abigail with a puzzled frown. "Why did you let him go?"

Abigail shrugged. Turning to walk back along the path to the house, she hugged her aching midsection with one arm, and tried not to limp. "Have you ever been hungry, Mr. Tarkington?" she asked as he caught up to her.

"Well, of course." He laughed, taking her elbow to assist her up the steps. "Before every meal—"

Abigail pulled her arm away, stopping in midstep. "I am not speaking of a hearty appetite," she said, looking at him directly since she was one step higher than he, at eye level. "I am talking about missing meals because there is not enough to eat."

He returned her gaze, his expression blank.

"Neither have I," she replied to his unstated response. Turning, she lifted her skirts daintily and started up the steps.

Matthew stayed put. "Preposterous!" he exclaimed heat-edly. "If you think Yasushi, or whatever his name is, goes hungry you are mistaken." He waved his arms about, indi-cating the abundant flora growing all about them. "If nothing else, enough bananas rot on the trees to feed everyone on Oahu." Taking two steps at a time, he caught up to her. "To be had for the picking, mind. Fish of every kind and description—"

"I do not say that he is personally hungry, sir," Abigail interrupted as he drew beside her. "I can, however, guarantee that he sends every penny of his wages to China. Who knows how many people are depending on him?"

Matthew was utterly amazed. Few girls of his acquaintance knew China existed, much less concerned themselves about famine. "You are the most perverse girl I have ever met," he cried. "Why worry your pretty little head about some place halfway around the world?"

"It is not China I worry about, Mr. Tarkington," Abigail said. "I worry about me."

"You?" Matthew was utterly bewildered.

"Me!" she exclaimed. "It was I who cost a man his job because of my tactless questions," she continued gravely. "I do not know how many people will starve because of my carelessness."

"But he was lying!" Matthew exclaimed.

"Was not his work of excellent caliber?"

"Yes, but—"

"And were you not satisfied with his performance until I began to meddle?" Abigail did not wait for an answer. "I daresay your sister will have much difficulty in replacing him. I do hope she will not be too angry with me."

"To the contrary, Miss Danforth," he replied, gesturing with his hand that she should take the more comfortable *punee*. "This will provide Penelope with dinner conversation for weeks to come. I assure you she will be most grateful on that account."

Abigail shook her head to politely decline his invitation to be seated. She would like to have reminded him how offended he himself had been by her inquisitiveness, but she had too much to do to prolong their conversation further. Nor was she free to tell him about his missing brother, who had been her only other real lead. "I fear I am doing more harm than good with my investigation regarding who might be poisoning you, Mr. Tarkington," she said, completely discouraged. "It would appear that I am not going to be able to heal you at all!" Before he could make a gratuitous protest, she added, "I seem to have twisted my ankle again. Would you perchance know where your sister keeps those miraculous ointments of hers?"

"Indeed I do," he said, concerned as much by her downcast demeanor as by her physical complaint. "I pray you, make yourself comfortable. I shall return before you can blink."

As good as his word, Matthew was hovering over her, jar in hand, before she had time to settle herself upon the *punee*. "This is what my sister has been using on me," he said, handing her a small jar. In an effort to cheer her, he added, "By the by, I visited a Chinese herbalist the other day. I wanted to see if he could give me a diagnosis."

"And did he?" Abigail asked eagerly, hoping to be relieved of her task.

"I could not ask him directly, of course," Matthew replied with a sigh. "He was noncommittal. He dressed my shin with an ointment," Matthew did not mention the tea since he had not bothered to brew it, fearing the smell. "I am to return next week."

"Do you feel any better?"

"At least I feel no worse." He shrugged. "And you, Miss Danforth? Might I ask if you feel well enough to ride?"

Abigail stood. "I am forgetting to tell you that I am due at the police station as soon as possible," she said, trying not to wince. "If I may prevail upon you to telephone a hack for me while I change?"

"Better still, I will have the boy hitch up the phaeton." He paused. Even though he realized he was being presumptuous, his curiosity got the better of him, and he asked, "Might I know why you are going to the stationhouse, if you do not mean to prosecute Yasushi?"

"There is the small matter of the man, I may now safely assume was Chinese, whom I left upon the mountain." Abigail blushed. "The police were to fetch him down. I was to come in and identify him. I told them I would be pleased to do so, after I had changed."

"May I be permitted to drive you?"

Abigail had had her fill of riding about unescorted. Since they were already scheduled to ride in the fields escorted by a *luna*, this change in plans, which would entail being surrounded by police officers, should cause Maude no distress. Especially since she had not yet returned from the Tibaults', and could not readily object. She therefore bestowed upon him a slight smile. "How very kind," she said, and repaired to her room where Jacqueline waited, her clean outfit at the ready.

There was no time to change corsets and examine the state of her midriff, although Abigail was much tempted to do so. Her ankle was another matter. It could not wait. Jacqueline swiftly unlaced the boot, and much to Abigail's relief, her ankle began to feel better almost at one. Jacqueline, however, insisted upon applying the cream, and did so, wrapping a bandage around it, more to protect the boot from being smeared than to support her foot. Abigail thought the cream had a different smell, but paid it no mind.

"If you will excuse me, miss," Jacqueline said, when Abigail's hat had been pinned in place. "May I fetch my hat and gloves and come with you? I have a few things I would like to take to Kinkade."

"I should have thought of it myself," Abigail said, only too pleased to have her act as chaperon, thus satisfying Maude's objections. "Do hurry," she added. "I am weary, and wish to retire early."

Jacqueline had no sooner closed the door than Maude opened it and entered, slightly out of breath. "What is this I hear?" she exclaimed, crossing to sit on the edge of the bed while Abigail remained seated at her dressing table. "Yasushi is Chinese?"

Abigail shook her head sadly. "It would appear so."

"Miss Tarkington is beside herself with fury," Maude replied. "She is insisting upon going to the police station with you. She says if you will not press charges against that— ah—lying heathen celestial—she will."

"Oh, dear," Abigail cried. "What have I done?"

"You did nothing, Miss Danforth," Maude said firmly. "It is Yasushi who lied. And if I understand correctly, he tried to have you killed." Standing, she held out her hand. "Come, my dear, I am going with you. It is about time I paid a call upon Kinkade. Perhaps together we can persuade him to recant his confession. The Tibaults have invited us to cruise with them on their yacht, which is a perfect solution to our travel plans. He must be free to join us."

Abigail groaned. She was already tired, but with Maude's reminder that she had not found the princess's killer either, she was suddenly so exhausted she could scarcely move. She felt a total failure, and ignored Maude's hand. Her face grim, she summoned her strength to gather her things and, with Maude holding the door open, she swept through it with a dignity she was far from feeling, and they hurried to the front lanai.

They need not have rushed. One of the matched pair had already been hitched to the phaeton, so when Matthew changed his request to the large carriage to accommodate everyone, the horse had to be unhitched, and the process repeated. With Abigail too depressed to talk, Maude curious but not daring to intrude, and Jacqueline unable to speak because of her lowly station, with the exception of Penelope muttering her outrage at Yasushi's betrayal, the ride was a silent one. It was almost dusk by the time Matthew parked the carriage on the side of the stationhouse and helped the ladies down.

Inside the stationhouse it was all Officer Miller of the enormous mustache could do to keep order among his men. Word of where Abigail's parasol had been placed in Shin's body had swept through the precinct. Every officer on duty, as well as a few who had lingered behind after their tour, knew she was due to come in, and all wanted a look at her. Shin's ninja star had also been found, which left no doubt as to his expertise. To a man, they dreaded confronting an Asian who was skilled in the martial arts. Too few survived. That a mere girl could have not only survived an attack unscathed, but killed her opponent—with a parasol—was a story none would readily believe. They wanted a look for themselves. That Officer Miller had assured them that she was no amazon, but a lovely, slim young girl, partial to fashion, and well connected to Honolulu's society, made the story even more incredible. So widespread was her fame that, the captain being off duty, Officer Miller had commandeered the captain's office for her use.

Discouraged, and struggling against her fatigue, Abigail was unaware of the sensation she was causing. She had been flat upon the ground with her eyes shut tight, had not witnessed the fate of her parasol, and was utterly unaware of being a heroine.

Following behind her, Maude and Jacqueline could not miss that every policeman glanced at Abigail, and although discreet, were whispering among themselves as she passed. Maude was glad that she had accompanied the young detective, the better to protect her, while Jacqueline was pleased with her choice of frock and hat, which her mistress wore with such style, and believed it to be the reason for all the admiring glances. While Abigail was shown to the morgue by Officer Miller, they were ushered into the captain's office, where Kinkade awaited their presence, uncuffed.

Matthew remained with his sister at the front desk while she filled out a complaint against Yasushi.

The amenities were scarcely done with between Maude, Jacqueline, and Kinkade, and the ladies, Kinkade, and his uniformed guard seated, when a pale and much subdued Abigail joined them, accompanied by Officer Miller. Kinkade shot to his feet, as did the guard and Jacqueline, who had taken a seat in the same room with Miss Cunningham only because not doing so would have forced Kinkade and the guard to remain standing. When all were seated again, Kinkade and Jacqueline upon the sofa, Kinkade's guard upon an upright chair nearby, Officer Miller in the captain's chair behind his desk, with Abigail and Maude in wooden armchairs in front, Officer Miller looked at Abigail and waited for her to speak. Two empty chairs near the door awaited Matthew and Penelope's arrival.

Death was not easy to look at, and Abigail was having much difficulty coming to grips with the damage her swat at a parasol had wrought. Her only desire was to quit the stationhouse, and Oahu, with all due speed and get on with her life, even though a cruise with the Tibaults sounded a dreadful bore. First, she must free Kinkade. There seemed one sure way to attaining his release, although it meant embarrassing herself in front of the two police officers. Steeling herself, Abigail ignored Officer Miller's obvious invitation to embellish upon her story of being attacked, and instead looked at Kinkade directly. "Did you know that Princess Lilliana was in the family way?" she asked.

"Miss Danforth!" Kinkade stood, his face in flames. "No! You cannot mean that!" He looked at his mistress, waiting for her to deny it.

"It is true." Abigail nodded, her voice firm.

Kinkade looked down at Jacqueline, then toward Abigail and Maude. "You surely cannot think that I—"

Officer Miller waved at the distraught man to be seated. "How did you find out!" he exclaimed. That the dainty girl who sat before him was so worldly amazed him.

"You mean you knew?" Abigail could hardly contain her surprise.

"Well, of course!" he exclaimed. "The autopsy clearly indicated—"

Abigail was outraged. "Why did you not tell me?" she interrupted.

"We thought it best not offend your delicate sensibilities, Miss Danforth," he replied smoothly.

"Why did you keep Kinkade in jail?"

"So as not to alarm the father."

"Do you know who he is?"

"Meaning no disrespect to the princess, we have been compiling a list. School chums, men who had been courting, or making formal calls," he replied. "We have begun some discreet questioning—"

"May I see the list?" Abigail asked.

Before Officer Miller could protest, the door opened and Matthew and Penelope entered. The men all stood until Matthew pulled Penelope's chair next to Maude's and she was seated. He then took the remaining chair by the door.

As Matthew was seating himself, Abigail was about to insist upon seeing the list when the pain struck. A stabbing pain, too great to bear, shot deep into the bone of her ankle. She gasped, and her cheeks lost color more swiftly than embarrassment had reddened them.

Officer Miller saw what was happening and was mystified. She had viewed the Asian's body with equanimity, and broached the most intimate question with aplomb, and he could not imagine what could cause her reaction. "Miss Danforth!" he cried. "Whatever is the matter?"

In thrall to the pain, Abigail could not speak. At that moment she would have willingly done anything to get it to quit. "That cream!" she managed to gasp when the pain subsided somewhat. "What was in that cream?"

"What cream?" Penelope cried.

"The ointment you use on my shin," Matthew said, bewildered by Abigail's reaction.

"You stupid fool!" Penelope exclaimed. "You had no right to go into my room!"

"But her ankle—"

The pain was bearable now, and Abigail found her breath. "Pray do not blame him, Miss Tarkington," she said, grateful that the pain had eased. "It is I who asked him to. The liniment you used last night had such a miraculous effect, I hoped for another cure."

"What if you got the wrong jar?" Penelope cried.

"How could I?" Matthew said. "I got the jar you always use. I should know it well enough by now!"

Feeling guilty for the quarrel between brother and sister, Abigail was about to protest, when the pain struck again. Again, she felt desperate, willing to do anything to rid herself of it. Is this how Matthew felt when he thought he had leprosy? she wondered. And then she knew. "It was you!" she exclaimed, pointing a finger at Penelope when the pain eased a little. "You poisoned your brother!"

"That is not true!" Penelope stood, her face blotched with anger. "How can you say such a terrible thing?"

The men got to their feet at once.

Officer Miller was completely bewildered by this turn of events, but he nonetheless signaled to Kinkade's guard to bar the door in case the large woman tried to flee.

"Every time you bandaged him, you poisoned him a little more," Abigail said calmly, despite her throbbing ankle.

"Why?" Penelope cried. "Why would I do such a thing? Answer me that? If Matthew goes to Molokai, I lose everything!"

Upon hearing the dreaded word, both police officers looked at each other, then suspiciously at Matthew.

"But if your brother committed suicide out of desperation, you would be a very rich woman," Abigail replied.

"You can prove nothing!" Penelope said haughtily.

"The jar of cream that your brother gave to me to use will be analyzed," Abigail said. "It will supply us with all the proof we need." Even as she spoke she knew such proof would be flimsy at best.

"Is this true?" Matthew cried.

Mouth grim, Penelope lifted her head defiantly.

Officer Miller could stand it no longer. "May I ask what a jar of cream has to do with Princess Lilliana's pregnancy?" he asked.

All of the defiance went out of Penelope. "How did you

know she was expecting?" she asked, suddenly looking as if she were about to cry.

Abigail was about to ask Penelope how she knew about the princess's condition when a possible answer that would tie everything together hit her as sharply as the pain in her ankle. But she had no proof whatever. Looking Penelope square in the eye, she did what she despised most in the world. She took a wild guess. "Is Bruce Dalton the father?"

Penelope lunged at Abigail. It took all of Matthew's and the guard's strength to hold her back. "He was going to marry the little slut!" she screamed. "After he promised me!"

"And so you killed her," Abigail said quietly, trying to keep the amazement that her guess was correct out of her tone.

"After all I had done for him, she was going to take him away!" Penelope burst into tears. Matthew relinquished his hold upon her so that she could get her handkerchief out of her reticule. The guard let go of her also, but stationed himself in front of the door.

Officer Miller thought he had seen everything. But this was too much. He did not believe one word of what he was hearing, and sounded like it when he asked, "And how, pray tell, did you kill her?"

Insulted by his tone, and not thinking at all clearly, between sobs Penelope described how she had followed Bruce Dalton and the princess to the pond. After he left it had been an easy matter to engage her in conversation, stick her with a poisoned hatpin, and, when the coast was clear, slide her body into the pond.

"One thing puzzles me, Miss Tarkington," Abigail said when Penelope was done. "Why did you particularly want me to find your brother Luke?"

"Humph! Think you are so smart?" Penelope blew her nose. "That should be most obvious of all."

"Ah, you are quite correct," Abigail replied. Events had unfolded so swiftly, she hadn't had time to think. She held a finger aloft as the answer occurred to her. "You would find a way to kill him also so that there would be no way anyone but you could inherit." Abigail turned to Matthew. "It would probably be a good idea to turn all of your father's medicines over to Dr. Stevenson for analysis. I will wager there are some potions among them that are not his."

Matthew was thunderstruck. He looked at Abigail in awe. "My word, Miss Danforth!" he exclaimed. "Pray do not take offense, but for a girl, you certainly can think."

"Hear! Hear!" Officer Miller chimed in heartily. "I second that, Mr. Tarkington."

Abigail scarcely heard their compliments. The pain had returned, and now that she knew the cause, she and Jacqueline hurriedly excused themselves to find a private corner where they could remove the offending cream.

While they were thus engaged, Kinkade took the opportunity to shake hands all around with his newfound friends. Taking Penelope's place in the carriage, he was pleased to learn that he would have Yasushi's room all to himself. "A phony, eh?" he said upon hearing the reason. With a smile, he added, "Rather like Diamond Head, I'd say."

"Now what am I forgetting?" Abigail asked, not expecting an answer although Maude stood in the doorway to the lanai. Kinkade had fetched the last piece of luggage, and Abigail was checking her room. "I must write William a note to thank him for saving my life. How churlish he must think me. And I shall enclose a check for the horse and carriage. The Messrs. Tarkington were so generous, I can afford to be."

"Are you going to tell Mr. Tarkington about his son Luke?" Maude asked.

"I think not, Miss Cunningham. Train tracks will meet before their paths will cross. It is the same with their ideas." She sighed. "It is not my intent to meddle in other people's affairs to no purpose."

Maude laughed aloud. "Miss Danforth!" she exclaimed

when she caught her breath. "How can you possibly hope to be a detective without meddling?"

"Some things are meant to be, Miss Cunningham," Abigail replied, offended by Maude's levity. "I do not wish to someday look back upon my life and discover that I have done more harm than good!"

"But there are times when you must interfere, Miss Danforth, if justice will be served."

"True enough." Abigail paused before continuing thoughtfully, "I only ask that I be granted the wit to perceive the difference."